"These are stories of individuals at a loss to deal with their lives. The apparently interminable nightmare of being stuck at wits end and the long dark process of reaching that point are summed up succinctly. The reasons for each character's failure are external... renewal becomes possible when the protagonists take within themselves a new responsibility for their own actions... the sometimes extreme escapes made possible in the final paragraphs come to seem like true redemption... the strength of these ideas struck me repeatedly in the days after reading them... this is a well crafted offering from a writer who appears to find the greatest of horrors in the suburban morass."

Duncan Lawie in *Touchpaper.*

"For atmosphere and mood I have seldom come across a story so rich as David Murphy's Uplands."

Roy Smith in *Vision (USA).*

"There's a subtle, humane quality... a sense that the author really is using his imagination and going beyond the obvious... a particularly fine performance."

Paul Beardsley reviewing *The Mirror Cracked* in *Interzone.*

"Murphy has a style of his own, and one that is definitely suited to the short story... Flying Kites and Broken Heroes are excellent examples of how short stories should be written, and are stories that would hold their heads high in any short story collection published today."

A *Robert Elliott* review from *First Contact.*

"Overload explores the life of a gay cross-dresser in post-millennium Ireland in poignant detail. The author's vision of a deteriorating social structure, a burgeoning population about to be controlled by mandatory abortion, and a growing authoritarian structure that is careening toward brutal abuse is compelling. Living in this murky mess, Ash, the protagonist of the story, is struggling to keep any bit of joy in this grim and grimy life. We wish him well, almost from the start, and yet we cannot see how wellness will form any part of his life. The story is a sigh, sad and sorrowful."

NV Berberick in *Tangent Online.*

"...the lyricism of David Murphy."

Olivia Hamilton in *The Irish Times.*

"David Murphy's fiction is so much more than promised. Stories too complex and too delicate to be explained away with a quick sentence, these are for quiet, uninterrupted reading late at night when everyone else is lost in sleep. Overload ... is the match of any short fiction that has been honoured with Hugo's or Nebula's or Stoker's. Every story carries its own unique brand of sorrow and regret. These are characters with no place to call home, nowhere to truly belong - the effect is devastating and arresting."

Lisa DuMond online at the *MEviews* site.

"Tasty comment on the current dumbing down that plagues our media-ridden lives."

Antony Mann reviewing *Oblivion Fade* in *The Fix.*

LOST NOTES

———————————————

To Dev

With All Best Wishes

David Munro

31/3/13

By the same author:
Arkon Chronicles (novel) 2003

Aeon Press, 8 Bachelor's Walk, Dublin 1, Ireland.
Text Copyright David Murphy (c) 2004.

ISBN 0-9534784-3-2

First published in the Republic of Ireland in 2004.
Set in 9pt Imperium - printed in Ireland by Ikon.
first edition

You can visit the author's website at:
http://gofree.indigo.ie/~dmbc/davidmur.htm

David Murphy

LOST NOTES

DUBLIN, 2004

Earlier versions of these stories were published in the following books and magazines:

"Broken Heroes", 'The Mirror Cracked", "Flying Kites", "Uplands" and "Lost Notes" appeared in the chapbook *Broken Heroes* (Albedo One Productions, 1995). "Lost Notes" was subsequently published in the anthology *Irish Short Stories 1996* (Phoenix). "Overload", "Something Small" and "Zoom-Time" were published in *Alienations*, a Pipers' Ash (UK) chapbook (1998). 'The Mirror Cracked", 'Walk With Me", "In Blueberry Hill" and "Overload" appeared in *Albedo One*; "Oblivion Fade" in *Electric Wine* and *Cold Print;* "Needs Want As Needs Must" in *Focus.* "Uplands" has also been published by *FTL, Dream Cell, Vision* and *U Magazine.*

CONTENTS

MIRACLE AT THE POINT

Her voice rasped past my ears like a whining bullet. "No!" she screeched, one of those breasts of hers squashing into my shoulder. She was bent over me, hand reaching for the controls. I reacted too late. She pulled the toggle so hard it broke.

"Wheel me back!"

"No. Serves you right. A rotten streak like you can't be trusted to go on automatic."

She yanked my chair hard to the left. A startled old codger jumped clean off the pavement. At least his legs were in working order. Bastard.

"You're some devil woman...!"

"Doesn't matter. It's a cheap old chair. Same as the rest of you."

I swore at her again, curses lost in the wail of passing sirens.

She was wheeling me fiercely. The racket-bucket was out of sight before I could tell if it was ambulance, fire, or cops. Who cares? Serves 'em right too, the whimperers and simperers who work here but live way out in the backyards of beyond. Here she is shoving me through a city whose citizens scuttle through streets like scared rats. I watched 'em run, the edifice of their lives tripping them up, dragging them down, entangling their feet, slipping and sliding them in their own rotten excrement. They tried to dodge past my advancing chair like shoals of herring darting around a moving shipwreck. I watched 'em swim with mouths open, scary-eyed, against the current. None of them had a clue where they were going.

I laid my head back and screamed, "Waa-hooo!" like a demented redneck at a C&W convention. I stopped yelling. If they're running out of town, where the f-

"I don't know why I'm doing this," she moaned. "Do you have to shout like a lunatic? This is not the time for shouting."

"Where are we going?" My backside fell several feet as she pushed the chair off a pavement. "That hurt! Use the ramps."

"We're in a hurry. No time for safe driving." Her voice had regained the matriarchal tone that said, 'I'm your carer. I'll look after you if it kills me'.

"Okay. But *where* are you taking me, Nur-" I caught my voice in time. The last day I had called her Nurse Ratched she brazenly upturned my coffee cup straight into my lap. Just out of the kettle, too. A sore lesson that not all her paperbacks were light romances. I thought better of making any more literary references. There was another high kerb. She was pushing like the Munster second row.

"We're going to the Point. If we don't hurry-" That voice of hers rose an octave as she shoved me off the kerb "-it'll be full."

I did some more astronaut training before hitting the seat with the force of several g's. "The Point! The bleedin' Point! So that's... Why?"

"We've got to hurry. I forgot to bring your notebooks."

Night fell around me like the mother of all whores. I'd

known for ages that she'd been reading my verses. What gave her the right to think I'd want to join those tossers down in the Point? The country had enough bad poets without me joining in. No use complaining to her. She was like the rest of them. Soon as things got tough, started running around looking for salvation. Some found it in prayer, in madness, in all day partying. Others, like Miss Panicky Two Shoes wheeling me along, think that a mass meeting of poets and musicians in the Point is a cool place to go. "Fuck," I mutter to myself as we go clanking on one of those arty-farty cobble-stoned pavements the Corpo never quite finished. "Fuck, fuck, fuck, fuck, fuck…"

"Sorry, hang on." She wheeled me onto the tarred road. We were going in a straight line now. Nobody came against us. No traffic except the shuffle of human feet, all marching in the same direction.

I looked at the river, at the subtle drawback of its watery knuckles. A flick of fingers, invisible to me, splashed gently in the night. The river had flashed me its come-hither wave many times. Tonight it flowed fast, and darkly suicidal. Many had opted for the warmth of its cold grip these last mad weeks. Its primordial soup strangely attractive, made for jumping into, to get away from it all… I tore my gaze from hypnotic ripples. Wind whipped up, watering my eyes, making the lamps on the far side look as if looping rays of light joined them, one to the other, like droopy telephone wires. The effect reminded me of my first joint. That was down here too, at a concert a long time ago.

A south side klaxon caterwauled me back to present tense. As that siren spiralled to its distant death, I heard another wailing in my ear:

"You have nobody to look after you, Vincent. The way things are, someone better look out for you. It's my job. I am your carer. Even if the service falls apart I won't abandon you. Caring is a vocation. I have no one else to worry about. Not since… well, you know…"

Yeah, not since hubby-dubby did a runner leaving a woman with a mission stuck behind my wheelchair. A vocation, for Christ's sake. What summed her up was the way she was always ringing her two aunts down the country. Even when martyring herself four afternoons a week looking after me, she found time to ring them - only from *her* mobile, mind. When the networks began to crack up a few weeks ago, forcing her to use my land-line, she insisted on paying for every call though I knew she was anything but flush. No wonder her husband had left her. God protect me from selfless, perfect women. Then the landlines went on the blink and the phone calls ended, which reminded me: "What about your aunties down the country?" I put on my concerned, pally-wally tone. "Bet they need looking after, Kate?"

"Can't visit them now, not with the transport system the way it is. Both of them are well taken care of in a home."

A Home for the Befuddled, no doubt. She was gliding me along with the strength that only a big wild culchie woman would have. Her rooster-red face and bossy red hair reminded me of nothing less than a bag of scrabbling weasels. At least she was behind me now, out of sight, pushing hard. Crowds were thickening. I tried one last tack.

"Why in Hell's name are you bringing me here? It's been four weeks since the last health board paychecks were issued. Home-helps haven't been paid since. Everyone knows that. Why are you still working?"

"You won't get rid of me that easily. I feel responsible for you, God help me."

We were nearing an appropriate place for such sentimental drivel. The Point loomed into view. A strange kind of silence fell upon the shuffling crowd, descending on my minder, too - no greater testimony to its potency could there be.

A cathedral to concrete, red-carpeted aisles - red seats, too. Blood and stone enveloped me, and seven thousand more, in regimented rows of willful hopelessness. Wouldn't you know, hatchet face arranged a place for us right in the middle of the auditorium. A mathematical wizard could not have picked a more central spot. She plonked herself down at the end of a row and pulled my chair against the armrest. "They're allowing chairs in the aisles tonight," she said, as if I was a child and this was a pantomime and that would make everything magically okay.

I could have screamed. I could have kicked up - figuratively, of course. I could even have wheeled myself out. I chose none of those things. The curiosity-seeker within me had taken over, empowering me to sit there and soak it all in. Call it voyeurism - that would be wrong. Tonight I was no voyeur - I was observer. Tonight within me lurked a willingness to let things happen, to wait and see, to watch. I waited as she arranged her scarf on her waist, layering it the way women do.

I looked all around, taking in the vast crowd. Distant faces, haunted, hung from tiered seats on the faraway sides of the concert hall. I looked at some of those faces. They were each the same, serried like lines of theatrical masks, grim and white, waiting for an execution. I felt myself surrounded by sad cases: the marginalised, the shallow-hearted, the emotionally disenfranchised, the Samaritan-ringers, the terminally pleasing, the empty-headed, the soap-addicted braindead, the nervously disenchanted, the middle-of-the-road, the game-show contestants. Behind me row upon row of losers sloped up and back to a sort of nothingness where dim spots shone down on the farthest of faraway heads. The rear end of the arena jutted out and up, a million miles over my head, making me dizzy, as if this was a huge aircraft hangar and I was a useless spanner lying in a pool of oil.

Lights dimmed. I raised my cranium from the back of the chair and looked straight ahead. Anticipation fell in heaps as darkness engulfed the audience. A single spot picked out the first performer. I recognised his familiar gait as he hobbled centre stage, a vagrant poet, icon of the homeless. The moment the audience realised who he was, they burst into loud applause. So typically patronizing. His poem was a staccato incantation. Every second line was the same. *The squeeze came, then the crash.* It rippled across the audience like a rhythmic pandemic. *The squeeze came, then the crash.* Effective, I must say - if a little tiresome. Then came music, acoustic and ancient, followed by contributions from well-known poets who were sitting in a ring around the stage. All the well-known ones were here: the stereotypically wild-haired, the sombre-suited, less exotic. They spoke and chanted, mainly about the economic crash. Some tried to whip up the audience by apportioning blame. Others rightly countered that that wasn't much use now. More music, from a performer at the side of the stage. All the more plaintive for being traditional, a conduit to times less dependent on technology, more self-sufficient, more innocent, perhaps. Whatever it was, it was played in a kind of vacuum as if silence itself had laid its physical presence somewhere down beneath our seats.

A man bounded out of his seat five rows back, centre aisle. Three leaps took him onto the stage, where he waved a piece of paper frantically above his head. Security men never let him get more than one step ahead. They pinned him down as he turned to the audience. *Bring him on, bring him on, bring him on*, roared the crowd, as if they were at a football match and he was a substitute warming up. Thanks to some neat footwork by the country's most popular poet - well known to the wider television audience on account of his performance-style poetry, though some might not call it such - an intercession was made on behalf of the man from the audience. He was allowed read his poem, a piece of soundbyte doggerel called *Schizophrenic Society*. Even before he was halfway through, dozens of poets were spilling out of the audience, limbering up for their moment of glory.

It was true, I knew, as if visual confirmation were needed, that the country possessed an army of poets. They were all here in the Point. I almost felt sorry for the hard-pressed security men. The side of my head sensed a nervous glance from the pair of eyes alongside me. A simple expletive cured her of any notion that I might want to be wheeled into the centre-aisle queue. Her eyes no longer burned into me, but were drawn to the stage where a celebrated Nobel Prize winner, though surely not for the versification that he gets away with, held his arms aloft. A messiah motioning for silence. "Let us recite our poetry together!" he urged.

The audience, unsure how to take such a request, turned in on itself in confusion. Even I looked agog at the Virago in the seat beside me. The poet repeated his bizarre request. Hollers of approval came from somewhere on my left. A ripple of applause broke loose on my right.

"He's right!" The performance poet was back in the spotlight, dancing eagerly around the Nobel winner. "Let's recite our work together!"

Applause grew. Queues of poets no longer jostled. They became orderly lines of men and women, also clapping. Above the noise, the two poets in the limelight began chanting in unison: "Let us recite our poetry together! Let us recite our poetry together!" The audience joined in, as did the other poets on stage, lending a rhythm to the chant that made it all the more deafening, all the more powerful. It was all I could do to prevent myself becoming part of it.

The poets on stage motioned for silence once again.

"On the count of three," said the Nobel winner. "It matters not how good our poem is. What matters is that it comes from our deepest soul. It may shed a light of spirituality in a declining material world. Let us recite our poetry together. Three poems each. No! Five! Our best five poems. Musicians, give us base phrases on which to recite. One. Two. Three!"

The on-stage poets stepped back from the mikes to prevent the crowd from mimicking their well-known verses. Members of the audience recited quietly at first, as if from shyness or deference to the person alongside them. I could have sworn I was back in church. What began as reticent cacophony, if there can be such a thing, might have petered out were it not for the music which lent a solidity to the mumblings, a structure on which voices grew louder, more confident.

I'm not sure how it happened. My voice took on its own life. Helplessly, I began reciting. Poets on stage held hands, as did the audience. The base drone of musicians remained audible behind the strengthening voices. Everyone seemed to be speaking, as if words were coming even to non-poets, if such persons were there that night, which there must have been. The millions of different words took on a jumbled clarity, gaining strength through difference, meaning through intensity, purpose through power of will. As if all the words took a sideways step through time and dimensions unknown to man, coinciding with a mysterious shuffling of hearts and souls. As if all the poets, despite their various backgrounds, colours, ages, sizes, ambitions, egos... As if all these things changed codes, the codes becoming some new kind of chromosome, vaguely organic, with a will of its own that rose tenaciously from the audience. I swear I saw it, felt it, rising from the crowd. It smelled of earth, cool and wet, and of fire. My throat went dry. I continued to recite. I even clasped the hand of the person alongside me, who was also speaking. What her words were I could not tell. We were well into our poems now. I looked up. I could feel the words gathering like overhanging tapestries, invisible ectoplasms of dynamic spirit. It was like a seven thousand-strong liturgy releasing raw emotion in the most sacred places of all those hearts, all those souls. A whirlwind was gathering, with a centrifugal force so slow it seemed to move not at all, yet possessing a centrifuge all the more powerful because of that. What began as theatre had become cathedral.

People were on their feet. Even Kate was standing, leaning

to one side so she could hold my hand. She was holding tightly. Something popped in the base of my spine. A surge of something shot me through with seven chakras worth of energy. I looked down. For a wild moment I thought I detected energy within my crippled legs. I tried to move them, hoping that I might rise from my chair and walk. It was not that kind of miracle.

When it was over, and everyone seemed to conclude their five poems at roughly the same time, it was like the end of the final curtain call after a particularly fine performance. People appeared satisfied and deemed it appropriate to leave. Poets walked off stage at the same time as the audience began filtering out, as if both were one and the same. The silence that had descended on the audience on their way in revisited them on the way out. Everyone, including Kate, was gobsmacked.

Nobody, myself included, is quite sure what happened that night. I long for clarity, for understanding, yet cannot even recall which of my own poems I recited. People have tried to repeat the performance of course. They have tried many times without the same... success.

They don't hold concerts there any more. The acoustics, never very good in the first place, have gone completely awry. Not that people worry about the sound problems. They're happy to leave it as it is, to congregate outside, to sing or recite poetry. It seems to attract a lot of wildlife - the Point, I mean, not the singing or the poetry. Birds flock to it and hover overhead, singing the sweetest songs. Fish gather at that part of the river and jump clear out of the water, as if saluting it. At night, though no lights burn within, its roof radiates a phosphorescent glow.

I never did meet Kate after that. My inability to communicate with her is something I regret. At least we parted on a friendly note. Therein, I believe, lies the key to the whole remarkable event. Whatever was released at the Point, and I do believe *something* broke loose that night, it enabled us to communicate in that final moment of parting. Its essence sits with me as I stare out my sitting-room window, re-living that amazing night.

Once again she wheels me, a silent Molly Malone, through the shuffling throng. We reach the quayside outside the concert hall. A weird sense of redemption hangs in the air. All are quiet, no one speaks. She pushes me along the tarred road up by the river, then back to my ground floor flat near the railway station. After the extraordinary event at the Point, our minds are in a jumble. I'm possessed of enough gumption to realise that something is different about her. I sense my voice returning. Knowing what is coming, I know better than to speak. At my hall door, she steps in front of my chair and tells me she will be leaving.

"I have things to do," she says.

"I know."

"I'm sorry about the controls on your chair."

"Don't worry. It's just the switch. I'll get it fixed tomorrow."

With a smile she turns to go. The shock of her bossy red hair, electrified by a nimbus of yellow street-lamp, highlights her in a way I never saw before. Her face is no longer a bag of scrabbling weasels. I see brightness behind her everyday skin. Her generosity shines like a halo. In her going I know that she too has changed and that I never will see her again.

"By the way," I call out, my throat still dry from the recitations.

She glances back.

"I never knew you wrote poetry."

BROKEN HEROES

The lough shone beneath a proud moon, a blue whale that stretched forever. Behind me, the hills of Donegal. The moon's rays were so pervasive the contours on those hills were plainly visible. Across the lough, on the southern shore, the main road. I could see it plainly though I wished I could not.

"It's 3am," was Conor's way of signalling that he was tired. And why not, I thought, for I was tired too.

"I know a place," I said, and I did, though I was tempted to sleep down by the memory-lapped shore. I had caught my first trout there, on a bubble float strung out with heather moths. I still see my father netting it for me. 'Step back as you reel in!' he said, afraid that I might lose it. He stretched and lifted out a fine one-pounder, big as the smile on his face. To a nine year old it was a monster that diminished not one whit in all the years and rivers and lakes my father and I had fished since. "Let's sleep in the sawmills," I said, "just over the hill, near the old army base. We'll be safe there for a few hours."

Thirty kilometres of tarmac had taken its toll on Conor. He laboured like a deep-sea diver beneath that rucksack. Me, I wore a duffle bag like a limpet on my shoulder. I pulled it tight as we crested a rise in the road. A hundred metres ahead lay the welcome refuge of sleeping logs. I was studying their perimeter fence when Conor tugged my sleeve. One glance at his face and I knew what was coming. "Car!" he hissed. Together we dived for cover into the roadside thickets.

Twin shafts of light cornered the road and speared the night. We cowered behind bushes, bending ourselves into invisible shapes. In a rush of noise and light the jeep passed by, oblivious to all but the floodlit road. We drank in its exhaust fumes before jumping out onto the tarmac - at least I leaped out. Conor eventually dragged himself and his infernal rucksack out of the bushes, but not before losing balance and almost toppling back. A long thorn in a sore place would have served him right, but funny it was not - he caught my disapproving look. By the time he was ready to walk, the red tail-lights had disappeared into the distance.

The timber yard was a sea of logs piled high in geometric rows. The stockpiles were layered, warm too as we discovered when we found a ledge, wide as a man, halfway up a pile of planks. Above head height, in the wind's lee, we stretched out happy as a pair of lumber rats.

I lay beneath my coat, gazing out over duffle bag-pillow at that old army base. I swore I could still see the oil stains of Chinooks and Saracens glistening on moonlit tarmac. The southern militia did not maintain even a skeleton garrison here now - no need to since the last of the Loyalists had long ago fled behind a re-drawn border. A rustle of paper caught my ears. Conor was sitting up, a single sheet in his hand. I wondered what it was he was trying to read in the night's dim light. Before

I got a chance to ask, he put the paper in his rucksack and turned to look at the skyline behind our log pile. Then I knew what he was thinking; his thoughts writ large as the Blue Stack Mountains so cruelly hidden by the crest of road above the sawmills.

Somewhere along that road we had forgotten to take one last look. Now it was too late. Donegal was gone; never to be seen again, though as far as Conor's resolve was concerned, I was beginning to have doubts. I too could feel the tang of Atlantic salt riding down on moonbeams over that crest; I could smell the turf from the slopes of Errigal on the breeze; I could hear, see, and taste those far-reaching charms - but I could not countenance going back. As I feared, Conor was beginning to wilt. One look at the brass mouthpiece sticking out of his rucksack and I knew that. He was also looking at that flute, and in his eyes I saw all the nights when father had taught us all those tunes. Those songs were playing for Conor now, calling him like a mermaid singing. "There must be a better way," was how he put it.

"No," I said. "We can't fight it here. We have to get out."

He was about to re-open that long argument but I killed it. "Best get some sleep," I said. "We've a long walk ahead of us tomorrow."

Four hours later an onsite chainsaw rasped a hostile wake-up call. In five minutes we were back on the road. By 9am Enniskillen beckoned. Our timing was perfect: plenty of people walked the road at that hour, which gave us cover from passing jeeps. There was no other traffic, the economic collapse meant fuel in these parts was reserved for the militia.

With my duffle bag over my shoulder I made an adequate impression of a work-bound brickie. My brother worried me though; he resembled a backpacking tourist - an exotic species around here. I looked ruefully at the lake on the right-hand side of town and thought of all the lakes that had once made this county so attractive. The lakes were still there, and just as pretty, but their spirit was different now. Something weighed them down and robbed their sparkle.

We could have taken a short cut via derelict Loyalist estates but that would have made Conor look even more of an oddity. Turning past the roundabout onto the Belfast road, I began to regret not taking that option when we found ourselves walking directly toward a pair of armed militia men. The stubby barrels of their weapons poked menacingly beneath threadbare flak jackets; one look at itchy fingers wrapped around those triggers made me want to pray - something I had not done in years. One look at Conor and I wanted to do something else - curse him from a height. Christ, getting out from under martial law was bad enough without waving a dirty great flag that says 'we are moving illegally from one part of the country to another'. That's what that bloody rucksack was: a flag, and Conor was waving it recklessly beneath their noses.

The sergeant had that fidgety look of the world-weary soldier. Indifference vanished when he looked into the rucksack. As for the private, his eyes stood on stalks when he saw the chocolate and the cling-wrapped salmon. Nothing like the sight of luxuries to make a raggle-taggle army man forget his orders. Conor rabbited on about the death of our father and the sale of the family home. It was all true; the militia men could have checked it instantly on their links but they were too busy salivating. They barely glanced at the papers I offered, preferring instead to take the salmon from Conor's outstretched hand.

"Why the hell didn't you tell me what you had?" I hissed as soon as we were out of earshot.

"You were moaning so much about the rucksack I just couldn't be bothered. It was a last minute decision - the oldest trick in the book: make 'em see what they want to see."

"Yeah? What happens if the chocolate doesn't work at the next checkpoint?"

"Then I'll show 'em the brandy and the expensive jeans."

That was too much. As soon as we turned the corner from the militia I stopped his cocky stride with a firm finger to the breastbone. "Listen," I said, "I've been around longer than you. They might be a run-down, half-starved scumbag of an army, but they're not all as thick as the two troopers we met back there."

"Gimme some credit," he was almost squaring up to me. "By the way, I've had this big brother routine up to here," he jabbed a finger at his collar, "and don't tell me how experienced you are. Fat lot of good it did our d-"

He stopped himself just in time. I swear I would have hit him there and then only for two things: half a lifetime counting to ten after most things he said, and the sound of an approaching truck. Creating a scene was the last thing we needed.

We trudged on a wordless road. Then we turned south for Lisnaskea. Our feet ached and as darkness fell we found a resting place. A semblance of civility returned between us.

"Just that one checkpoint," said Conor. "Things are looking up."

"We were lucky," I said. "We still have a long way to go." I knew then that he would say it would be safer the further east and south we went, and I knew too that this was another signal that he was reconsidering our decision, so I added, "They're going to take over the whole country, Conor. Best get out before it gets too bad."

"You always look on the bright side." He smiled up at the stars. Then he looked at that brass mouthpiece sticking out of his rucksack. For a moment I thought he was going to play a tune. Talk about attracting attention. Before I could say anything he was turning the other way. "Clover for sheets tonight," he said. "Sleep tight, brother."

But I could not sleep. The stars were pinpricks jabbing my eyes. When I closed them I saw again that mob at my father's gates, baying like hounds for the kill. It had not started like that, of course. First it was a picket line - all frosty looks and stony silence. Then silence gave way to slogans, and stones became real enough to break windows.

Father was always going to be an easy target. He had made the mistake, years before, of refusing to teach religion. Teachers had that option in liberal days. Then the European Union collapsed, the British pulled out of the north, and chaos ensued. When the dust settled, the Loyalists had their fortress in the northeast. Militant nationalists had everywhere else. At first their so-called protective measures were designed to turn the country in on itself. Foreign broadcasts were jammed, liberal publications banned - so too were satellite dishes. E-mail and networking were outlawed, making computers illegal, except government ones which held files on state employees - files with information like, 'opted out of religious instruction'.

It became serious in rural areas first, especially the northwest. Father had been retired for years, but moral cleansing deals with sins of the past as well as the present. When the local mullahs named him from the pulpit of St Declan's, he should have sold up and moved out. But father was stubborn as a deep-diving salmon. He had lived all his life within a long cast of the Atlantic and was not going to move now. Then the pickets came, and when stones broke his windows righteous hands reached in and hauled him out. That was when Conor and I broke the travel laws and came up from Dublin.

I see him now in that musty courtroom, eighty years too clearly etched on his sunken face. On the day of his retirement, he had calculated that he had put fifteen hundred children from the parish of St Declan's through his hands. Given each of them six hours a day for a whole school year. He used to joke about the responsibility of 'terraforming people's minds' as he put it. I see him now, stooped and bent in anguish that all the civilization in the world could be nullified by a kangaroo court. I see him staring red-eyed as the local puppets performed verbal trick-of-the-loops, intellectual bungee-jumping like 'No teacher should have to teach religion but every teacher should want to'. I see him shake his head incredulously as those around, including some he had taught himself, nodded their heads in approval. That's what killed him in the end - the realisation that his life's work had been in vain; that those he had taught could turn out like this.

After what seemed a mere half-hour of sleep my nostrils twitched to the aroma of early-morning coffee. Conor handed me a dew-dripped mug. Nothing ever tasted so good. I sipped and watched him rub ointment on his blistered feet. He offered me some but I declined. Less than five hours separated us from Cavan. Blisters could wait until then.

Cars became more frequent the further south we went, jeeps less so. Fuel was not so scarce down here; affluence not yet as decimated as it was further north. By mid-afternoon we hobbled into Cavan. Yellow and white bunting across the streets told us we were passing through not a moment to soon - there was to be a religious retreat that weekend. We exchanged rueful glances. Retreats were invariably followed by outings like the outing of our father.

Past the church we walked, where a sanctified woman on bended knee scrubbed the entrance clean. She lifted her gaze to us, her hands never leaving the granite slabs. She washed away the sins of generations, removing forever the last vestiges of impurity. Her eyes met mine and I knew she could see into my soul. Her hands still scrubbed but her lips broke into the worst kind of grin: the shady grin of one who had never known power, but was empowered now. I broke eye-contact with her as quickly as I could, hoping she would not notice the bandana of sweat that had sprouted on my forehead. She kept scrubbing, and I hoped she remained at her pious task as we strolled into the bus-station, trying to look casual.

The ticket clerk had the servile smile of a parasite. His beady eyes took us in from head to feet, then back up again via Conor's rucksack. "Under new travel law restrictions," he smiled with cobra-like sincerity, "I can't sell one-ways to strangers - not unless they have special clearance. Do you get my drift?"

Bill-of-sale papers from father's cottage were not enough to deflect those snake-like eyes from the rucksack. The man's body language stated articulately that the local economy had reverted to its more traditional form - barter. We understood alright: the brandy produced the desired result.

Twenty minutes later we were on our way, never so grateful that public transport still existed. This was drumlin country - all rolling hills and undulating road. No place for walkers. Not that we would have been able for much more. My blisters were Himalayan now. I had to use some of Conor's ointment. Of course he had to chirp that if I had used it earlier my feet would not have hurt so much. I complimented him on his excellent hindsight. We journeyed on in silence. I looked out at passing hills - anthills compared to the hills of Donegal.

After the court appearance Conor tried to talk father into moving to Dublin. I argued against it - an old man needs his self-respect. Conor retorted that I was confusing self-respect with pride. He would say that.

Within days of returning to the cottage, back to broken windows and stone-littered floors, a new directive advocated the rounding up of 'agents detrimental to the common good'. Politicians, legislators and media people were incarcerated throughout the land. Not many of them lived in Donegal, so local militants sought other targets. Father, for instance.

A streetful of moral coat-tail riders gathered outside the narrow slits of already boarded-up windows. They stood there chanting; their nightmare howls bending truth and light, darkening an already darkened landscape. They cast history-warping stones and hurled fact-shifting rocks. An army of blind-faith soldiers bent on obeying orders of obedience, and enforcing them. A Holy Crusade of men - Guardians of the Faith; women - Queens of Heaven; and children - no gilt-winged Angels of Innocence, these.

Their sledgehammer dogma broke down doors. Anger swam in father's eyes. His face checkered with blood pressure as he bellowed at the splintering wood. On his feet, then off his feet, he keeled over clutching his chest.

The leader of an army of rectitude stood in the hallway, nonplussed by the body stretched before him. He knew not how to harangue a corpse. His confusion became alarm when he saw what came through the air at him. Conor vaulted over the table; a slow-motion vault that took him clean over every one of father's eighty years, over each river and lake he had fished, over every song and story he had told. A vault, inspired by the death of an old man, that sought out the death of another. Conor was thwarted as the invading mob fought him off and pinned him to the floor.

I made myself a buffer between them. I took punches meant for him. I pulled him clear. I pleaded for understanding. Conor crawled free, fists still clenched. Father lay on the floor, a piece of paper in his death-unfurled fingers.

The journey from Cavan to Dublin was long. Time slowed the way it does when Lady Luck deals you a rotten hand. Then it stopped altogether like when the deathcard lands in your lap. Or to be more accurate, when it steps onto the bus wearing a militia badge, when it walks with slow and deliberate pace to the seat behind you, when it leans forward and says, "Do you mind if I ask you something?"

I saw the alarm on Conor's face. In his eyes I saw my own fear reflected. My head spun with the dreaded possibility that the militia man was about to check our travel permits, to order us off the bus. I knew how Conor would react to that, and I saw all that we had achieved in getting this far thwarted. Then the militia man said, "Could you spare a servant of the country a couple of coins to help him on his way home?"

I heard slurred words and smelled alcohol. Time marched forward again. The militia man thought we were smiling because we were happy to help him. He was wrong; our smiles were carved of bottomless relief. At Navan we again watched him walk slowly and deliberately - into a roadside bar. Our bus pulled away. We looked at each other and I slowly shook my head. Conor let out a long, low whistle. Wheels turned fast as we travelled the last leg of our journey in silence.

Dublin was almost different. Motorways, tolls, and feeder roads gave the impression of a new-millennium city. In the suburbs the mask slipped to reveal the burned out, bombed out husks of factories. When road turned to street and the bus slowed, we saw the faces of passers-by. Mean faces they were, the question mark of what went wrong scribbled in blood on their brows; weighing them down, haunting them, burying them in their recent sad history. Grimness, fear, rectitude - these were our welcoming committee as we drove into town. And sirens. Sirens that rang not to pipe us off the bus, but to herald the closure of bookshops under new censorship laws.

We walked past bridges of hopefuls trolling the snot-green river for mullet, the latest substitute for fresh meat. Along the quayside, whores on the early shift leaned against dark alleyways like off-duty soldiers relaxing at barrack walls.

Another bus took us to Conor's flat. It had been raided. Books littered the floor, their titles undoubtedly noted for some preparatory book of evidence. By a pre-arranged signal we said nothing for fear of bugs. Conor filled the empty spaces in his rucksack with the bits and pieces he deemed essential. From his window I watched for militia. From his other window I saw the ferryport and the park. I pointed at the park.

We sat on a bench, a great willow flapping against our backs. Before us, through the rusty bandstand, the upper decks of the ferry shone swan-white, the only gleaming thing in an otherwise decaying harbour.

"I'm not going," he said.

"I know. What will you do instead?"

He took the flute from the rucksack and let his fingers hover over the holes. He shrugged and said, "There's a safe house not far from here."

"You're a foolish man."

"At least I'm not a coward."

"Don't talk rubbish. You're playing into their hands by staying. You're letting anger rule your head. It's not cowardice to pull out - it's common sense. Go abroad, organise, fight them from a distance at first. They've too much control here now. They'll sweep you up tomorrow morning and throw you in jail, if you're lucky. Lay low until the mood of the country changes. When they become even more oppressive, when they've hurt too many people, there'll be plenty of others like you. Then begin the fight."

"Lay low?" he snorted. "That's exactly what you did when they came for our father."

I glared at my own flesh and blood, counted like mad, and said, "I pulled them away from you."

"Yeah. Protecting them."

"You're full of shit, Conor. Poisoned by hatred. If you don't cop yourself on you'll do something stupid and they'll have you in a flash."

"And you'll do nothing. Just walk away from it all like it never happened."

"You're being an idiot," I said.

He whipped open a side-buckle on his rucksack, snatched

out a scrap of paper and held it under my nose. "What the fuck is this?" he said.

The Gates of Heaven, St Declan's Cemetery. Padlocked to all but the faithful departed. Father's coffin ached into our shoulders as the caretaker refused to open the locks. "Declan's is consecrated ground," he said. "Reserved for true believers."

The weight of my father shifted as Conor stepped from one foot to another. Anger boiled in him like magma spurting from somewhere deep, somewhere sacred. It roared through his shoulders, rippled through the coffin, and percolated down my spine where it met, and matched, the hot blood rising in me. Two things saved the caretaker from being buried in his own graveyard: a large squad of militia standing at the gates, and the dignity of my father's final journey.

Behind the boarded-up windows and battered door, in the stony soil of common ground, we buried him. The local estate agent, a man seedy and haggard through lack of business, stood at the graveside before offering us a pittance for the cottage. We took it. Time to cut loose, to scuttle the boat.

I see that cottage now, and the grave behind it. I see it clear as the scrap of paper in Conor's hand - that same piece of paper he had stared at that night in the sawmills, the paper crunched up in my father's dying hand. It was the purchase docket for a plot in St Declan's Cemetery.

"Father's last wish." Conor spat the words into my face. "Despite it all, he wanted to be buried in Declan's. He bought the plot six months ago. They persecute even the dead. And you're going to let them away with that? I'm not. I'm going to stay and fight, and organise here. And if there's no one else I'll still fight. And if they jail me or kill me, so be it."

My country ebbed from me in a swirling wash of mud. I clung to the side-rail, ship's noise shuddering through hands and feet and stomach as the screws pushed the pier away. Above it all a sound; a familiar trill of notes soaring above the cacophony of busy harbour and departing ship. No cruel blast of horn, no squawk of gull, no squeal of emigrant child, no belch of engine, could match the long weeping notes that floated across the dock, over the water, into my ears, into my head. I could see a tip of willow above the park. The music came from deepest willow roots. Though I could not see him I knew he was there, sitting on the bench, playing that distant tune of a distant land. A land, a tune, that grew ever distant, ever fainter, yet was still audible above the din of ship and shore.

I closed my eyes and heard that tune a hundred times a year for thirty years. Then I listened to it one last time and thought of Conor and all the fights we'd had: one for every note. I waved to where that willow was, or where it approximately was, for the ship was turning now and the park was growing smaller. I waved to him one last time and wished him well. When they caught him and took him to where they took people like him, he would, I hoped, have plenty of time to play that tune, and to teach it to others, and never let it die.

THE MIRROR CRACKED

There was the moment of flux, the meta-moment. Dorothy closed her eyes not wanting to see the transformation in the mirror. Enough that she could feel it. Often in the past she had stared, but not now. She couldn't bear to look now.

The molecular shift, subtle at first, crept across her face. Her skin loosened then filled as flesh crawled and bone expanded. Her skullcap tingled. Sprouting follicles lengthened her hair, bleaching it the colour of sun-drenched straw.

Dorothy opened her eyes. The result was pleasing, definitely pleasing. She pouted lips that were now full and red, but not red enough. Mentally mouthing the command 'make-up: typical', she watched her lips tremble as if hungry ants were crawling all over, kissing them crimson. With the reddening and the tingling they twitched and pouted even more, making her look just like the real Marilyn.

Dorothy slowly shifted her gaze to her babydoll eyes. Flawless, bluebell eyes. Her gaze lingered on them. In their blue pools she saw subtle hints, ripples of hope and expectation. For a moment she thought she saw something else: a sheen of innocence glistened back at her but was gone in the twinkling of a wet eye. It was a cry for love, for contentment. Whether it was her own longing glistening through or some crazy, contradictory innocence exuding from the real Marilyn, she could not tell.

An innocent, emotional Marilyn looked good - guaranteed to appeal to the client's noble, protective instincts. Dorothy held her breath, hoping, believing her look would trigger the desired response, so that when the light above the mirror turned red she felt ever so deflated. When the sign below the mirror flashed 'Archtypal Rubenesque' she was surprised. The twentieth century, with all its garish variety, was Xavier's favourite. He rarely strayed from his usual patch, almost never going back before Isadora. Dorothy consoled herself that the change to Rubenesque would not be too difficult - Marilyn was chubby enough already. Little alteration was required, just a gentle filling out. She felt her cheeks puff up slightly, though she was aware that most of the filling out was going on down below. A wave of energy brushed her hair, sweeping it back, darkening it. A gentle change, not too much, not too demanding, but unlikely to appeal to Xavier.

The light did not wait long. Dorothy expected it to go red, but when the sign beneath flashed 'Twiggy' she cringed. Talk about extremes. She sighed. When a client pays top-dollar, he gets what he pays for.

This time the meta-moment stretched like an hour - an elongated, never-ending, tortuous twist in her mind and body. Her whole being condensed. Bones shrunk and skin shrivelled in a quick slow-death. Diminishing in stature, in dignity - she had long ago learned to live with that - she felt herself creaking, contracting into a matchstick. She could almost feel her inner organs crumble in an anorexic miasma. Like dying of old age in an instant, she thought.

Metamorphosis over, she opened her eyes and looked in the mirror. Her hair was yellow again, yellow as flowers in a Van Gogh painting, and short, very short. But her eyes, Jesus. Big and round and misty again. Dorothy tried not to look coy. Xavier hated the coy look. She knew that and hoped this wasn't a run through her entire late twentieth century blonde short-hair catalogue, Twiggy to Diana to Madonna to... A lot of clients liked the vampish Madonna look. Dorothy hated it because it made her feel even more like a scrubber. Inevitably with a lot of customers, it led to Archetypal Punk. If there was one thing Dorothy could not stand it was the disgusting sensation of rings or pins bursting from her nose. She much preferred the dark, sultry look. The Magdalene was her favourite.

The flashing sign broke her from her reverie. She looked down and shook her head in disbelief. He couldn't want that again, not after the last time. Her incredulity gave way to a numbing sense of the inevitable. She heard herself say, "That's gonna cost you more."

"How much?" said the voice behind the mirror.

"A thou."

"That's twice as much as last time."

"Takes a lot out of a girl. You want it, you pay."

For a moment nothing happened. Then a thousand credits flashed onscreen, followed by that nauseating instruction. Dorothy looked down at it as if staring might make it disappear but it didn't. First she saw the hyphen, then her focus expanded and into her consciousness seeped the word 'Self-assembly' with all its implications. There was nothing to do now but stand there and wait for her client to begin.

It was her hair first: lengthening and reddening. Then the cheekbones: higher. Not knowing what to expect next, Dorothy felt her nose expand. She remembered the last time; it was the same: hair, cheekbones, nose and... Lips? Yes, fuller again. Lines of marching ants again, in her eyes this time, turning them... Brown? Yes, brown. She was afraid to open them, to look until the process was over. When she thought it might be over, it started again. Minor adjustments: eyebrows, beauty marks, curls; lips again, eyes again; then the neck - stretching - and the shoulders - squaring out - and the arms - elongating - and the rest... Then back to her face: forehead, chin, nose again. Why spend so long on her nose? Longer than the last time, that's for sure. No way would she put up with this if he wasn't such a regular...

The red light changed to green, the mirror slid slowly into its slot in the ceiling and Dorothy stood before her client.

"I'd prefer if you'd get dressed," he said.

Xavier was rare: a client who didn't care for sex. Rarer still, he was a client who preferred her with her clothes on. Dorothy valued him for that and valued him too because he made her feel useful and wanted in ways other than the obvious.

She dressed languidly, wondering who she now was. Xavier, still on the other side of where the mirror had been, stared at her with eyes wide and wistful. When she asked, "How do you want me to speak?" he said, "Don't say anything. Don't say anything at all."

"Okay. Just tell me what you want me to do."

Her voice made Xavier wince but he recovered quickly. "Nothing really," he said. "Would you like to go for a walk - for an hour? Is a thousand enough for an hour?"

The last time he hadn't spoken at all, hadn't even raised the mirror. Just sat there staring, silent and transfixed, until his time was up. Now a plaintive quality in his voice touched her to the marrow. It was a plea that despite its unusual nature she could not refuse. She nodded, put on her coat and together they left the booth.

Out on the street Xavier said, "Toss back your hair, please."

She did, and smiled, and in that moment saw in his eyes that she was no longer Dorothy but a long lost love that reached down at Xavier's heartstrings and pulled them so hard she could see he was visibly hurt.

"Let's go out along the bridge," he said.

Avoiding teeming streets they took the short route down by the Port Authority, along the river. Occasionally, he asked her to toss her hair again. Sometimes she did it of her own accord, which made him happy and made her think how easy, how inviting, it would be to slip into another personality, another life. She wanted to ask him who, and why and when and where, but she did not want to spoil it by speaking. At the bridge he said they should walk out to the middle before looking back. That way the sunset would be more... magical, he said.

He was right. The effect was startling. A blood-red sky interfaced with the rising silhouettes of skyscrapers; the skeletal bridge was caught in a golden sunburst that lit up its latticework like a bridge in wonderland. Dorothy tossed her mane again, not consciously this time, and looked at Xavier.

He was staring down over the parapet. A globe of a tear, golden in the sun, rolled down his cheek and fell into the greater mass of water below. Dorothy's gaze followed his tear for a hundred metres until it met the great river. When she saw the cold, relentless tide she felt dizzy. When she glanced at Xavier and saw the look on his face, and looked down at the water again, she felt scared.

"Let's go," she mumbled, half-expecting him to protest, to reach out. He merely glanced at her and quickly turned away but she had seen the wet rims of his eyes. Between her thinking how relieved she was that he hadn't lunged and thrown her off the bridge, and how sorry she felt for him, he said, "Yes, the hour will be up by the time we return."

Down by the bridge they walked, past the Port Authority, along the river. She did not toss her hair again. Xavier would not have noticed anyway. His head was bowed, too wrapped up in his personal cloud of melancholy. He had come to her so often, never for anything other than to look, to talk, to work through her catalogue. He had always exuded an air of sadness, of love unrequited, yet not once had he hinted of anything in his past, except for the last time when he asked for the 'Self-assembly' option. That was when she first realised the depth of his loss. She looked at him now. He was bent forward as if a riding crop was forcing him to keep in front of her. His centre of gravity was all wrong as if he was leading into some mysterious headwind that kept her from seeing his face even in profile. Yet he did not abandon her. He stayed by her side all the way back to the seedier part of town.

Past the ghetto they walked, past childhood's doors, past streets of shame, past gutters and kerbs that had blown away her hopes and broken all her dreams. She remembered it all now. How it began, how it never stopped. It surrounded her like a lead weight crawling, swelling around her heart.

By the time they stood on the sidewalk outside the brothel Dorothy could contain herself no longer. "What's wrong?" she asked in a voice she knew would now be even more painful for him. "Tell me what's wrong."

"It's your face." He glanced up the street, down the street, anywhere but at her. "I can't get the face right. There's something... It's the nose..." He shrugged. "...My memory, I guess. After all these years..."

"I understand." She wanted to reach out, to hold him, but all she could say was, "Next time you'll get it right."

"Yeah, sure. Thanks anyway." He turned and walked away. In the turning and the walking she knew she would never see him again.

The mirror slid slowly down on a woman once loved, always loved. Dorothy wondered how long ago it had been, and if she had loved him too. It would not have been difficult to love a man like Xavier, but she didn't even know the woman's name or if she was still alive. If only Xavier had a holograph he could get her face right. Then...

Dorothy could not keep them down, these hollow promises from a past unfulfilled: chances not taken, gambles unwon, mistakes best forgotten yet unforgettable. Life's lost opportunities rampaged like furies through her heart. She wanted to scream until the mirror cracked but all she could manage was a sigh - and that rumbling tremor came from somewhere so fundamental it barely registered by the time it escaped her mouth. He didn't even have a photograph, not even a faded, dog-eared, old-fashioned picture. She looked in the mirror at that lost face and thought it cruel that it should come to this for Xavier, for her, for whoever owned that face. Her eyes grew misty once more, and as the tears welled up the light turned red. Another client stood behind the two-way glass. The sign flashed and Dorothy began to change again.

Overload

Ash stood on the widest bridge in the biggest city in Ireland. He leaned on the parapet, the parapet of life itself, and stared down. Crazy boat races and swimmers and mermaids came first, then the entire Liffey turned black as Guinness, a vast river of stout flowing down from St James' Gate. It hit a weir in front of the bridge, spouted up into the air, and arced down into Ash's happy expanding mouth. Then the river turned brown as turds hit the back of Ash's throat. He spat them out and saw the river running red now from blood and corpses. Vikings flowed by, and Normans and Iron Age hut-dwellers and dozens of British soldiers and Irish freedom fighters. Bodies of mugged tourists collided with corpses of stabbed prostitutes. A wide-eyed country girl floated by, naked from the waist down. Her eyes stared up, pleading, trying desperately to understand why this was her first and last glimpse of Dublin. When she was swept away under the arches the river grew calm and Ash saw again something his father had taken him to see back when he was a child.

It was a clock, an incredible millennium clock. It floated under the water; a series of nine numbers counting down the seconds to the end of the twentieth century. Ash vaguely remembered the clock from sitting high on his father's shoulders and looking down over the parapet. The clock did not last long - the Corporation had forgotten to put wipers on it and soon it became covered in slime. In the end it was taken to wherever failed clocks go. Not that anyone cared about it the night of the millennium. The crowds went wild, bands played and everyone sang. Fireworks cracked and split the sky.

Here was Ash many years later and the millennium clock rose and fell once more with the Dublin tide. Its fiery-green digits pulsed away the numbers again, only now it was a tide every second as all the millennia of tides that had ever ebbed and flowed in the course of this great river flowed again in the final seconds of vanishing time. As the last digit went to zero Ash felt the weight of the whole world bearing down on him, yet nothing ever felt so light. He laughed and glanced sheepishly around, expecting everyone who happened to be on the bridge to be staring at him. It was busy yet no one seemed to be looking Ash's way. He laughed again. Whether anyone noticed him was the most important thing in the world and also the most trivial. Semi-aware now of reality, Ash realised he had been away forever and come back in an instant. It had been sensually celibate, crazily sane, side-splittingly serious and totally unlike any other trip he had been on before.

He was down now. His watch told him he had less than an hour to the evening shift; barely time to change out of his tight skirt and high heels to make himself presentable for work in a most respectable bar.

Ash's long hair straddled his ears. Premature greyness gave him the look of forty rather than twenty. His limp mop-top, silver and straggly, reminded people of that mad-cap professor from those time-hopping sci-fi movies popular back at the corner of the century. Ash was sick of the comparison but he smiled at the thought that those long grey tresses were a guaranteed man-killer whenever he dressed up for a night out with the girls. He glimpsed his smile in the huge gilt-edged mirror behind the counter, the mirror bearing the legend, 'Conan's Contemplative Bar'. Beneath that legend a line of fine gold lettering: 'Conan Milligan, Purveyor of Fine Wines and Spirits'. Something else was in the mirror: two shadows, moving. Ash turned around, recognising the two figures stepping into the lounge. One of them was short and fat. The other walked with the air of one who had seen it all and done it all - several times. They walked over to the counter and looked him up and down in that dismissive way of theirs. The younger one - the short fat one - asked, "Where's the boss tonight, Ashley?"

Ash knew that Milligan was spot-checking the nearest Contemplative Bar, less than two minutes walk away. He hated it though when anyone called him by his full name, except when he was dressed up. He had another hate too, the police, so the name he gave the two officers was Conor's, the most remote pub in the hugely successful Milligan chain.

"Thanks, Ashley," the policeman said. They both turned to go. Ash could see one of them - the older one, the silent one, the one whose name was Cluskey - shake his head as they walked out. Ash also caught the sneer on the side of Cluskey's face as something snide slid out of the corner of his sidekick's mouth. Ash did not catch it all but he heard enough to recognise the sentence as *Where does he get them from?* The remark did not upset Ash too much; he permitted himself another smile at the prospect of their wasted journey. Of such childish pleasure revenge is made.

Five minutes later Conan Milligan walked into the bar.

Twenty minutes after that his mobile rang. He spoke briefly. "Sorry about that, Superintendent Cluskey," he said, glaring across the floor at Ash. When he had re-directed the police officers he accused Ash of deliberately giving wrong information.

"I gave the right name, Boss. You know how people confuse the names sometimes." Ash shrugged his shoulder and loaded the washer. Confuse them they did, but the names had become a huge advantage when it came to marketing strategy.

Conan Milligan had happened upon a crock of gold in early twenty-first century Ireland. The gold was a pub in a fashionable area of Dublin; a pub no different to many others - a busy, noisy, bustling place. Milligan, countryman with country ways, disliked the noise and the clientele. He set about transforming it into something different. The new owner had a nose and a half for business, and a willingness to take a chance. He went beyond a smoking ban by prohibiting jukeboxes, radios, mobiles (except his own) and all screens from the widest wallscreens to the tiniest laptops. Media advertisements stated that groups of more than four were not welcome. Party-goers and revellers were encouraged to go elsewhere. 'Conan's - a quiet, conversational, contemplative bar' - so ran the initial ads.

First it was the after-workers, those stressed-out refugees from the hundred miles-per-hour whirlwind of modern life. Lost souls, out of step and out of time with the frantic march of progress, they stood on Milligan's doorstep like Trappists at the monastery gates. They came to shake off the cares of the world. They came singly, clutching newspapers and books. They came to lose themselves in crosswords and escapist yarns. Most of all they came to savour quietness, tranquility, absence of noise. They seemed to have no homes to go to, or chose not to go to them, at least not for an hour or two. In an age of sensory overload Conan's became their haven. They came to unwind, to debrief their minds of the endless info-dumping that bombarded them at work, at home, in the media, in the street. They did not drink at a fast rate but they came in numbers. They came between-work and out-of-work too, and at all times of the day and night.

Others came in twos and threes, quiet conversation their magnet. It was tacitly understood that the surroundings and the clientele were not conducive to loudness. People were attracted by the ambience of dim light, tranquility and good chat. Like moths to a flame they came out of the dark clutter-dense culture that seemed to stop at the threshold of Conan's Contemplative Bar. They came to hear themselves think and to hear their companions speak without having to strain their ears. Milligan encouraged these groups. He used the rule about groups of four merely as a publicity ploy, for he knew that the hum of good conversation leant itself to an increase in the consumption rate. He was smart enough to close the doors before the pub was full - comfort was paramount. When Conan's Contemplative Bar was turning them away every night he opened another - Conal's Contemplative Bar. It was also lined with bookshelves. It too became a popular haunt. 'Conan's or Conal's - in either you'll hear it right' - so ran the ads. Next came Conor's Contemplative Bar, where the only loud noise came from the constant opening and closing of the cash register - music to Milligan's ears, music equalled in later years by the swish-wipe of debit-cards in a society that went cashless in its mad dash into the twenty-first century.

Like most popular venues, Milligan's also attracted the wrong sort of clientele. Trendy journalists, fashion junkies and such like - wrong customers of the shallower kind. Unfortunately, when the novelty surrounding the bars wore off, they began to attract wrong ones of a deeper, more sinister hue. One shark that swam in both ends was the politician. Ash could barely abide the basking types, but the great whites that jumped in at the deep end made his stomach churn. In their cold dead eyes and sharp white fangs Ash saw dangers everywhere, yet he served them drink and served it with a smile. He served their pilot fish too - policemen like Cluskey. In new-millennium Dublin jobs were hard to come by and even harder to hold. Now that Ash had one he was not about to give it up. He had it all figured out: Milligan's conservatism, allied to the reactionary nature of the concept behind the contemplative bars, led to a clientele that was authoritarian and right-wing. That was Ash's analysis of his workplace and its customers. Take the two policemen for instance. Their wild goose chase had eaten forty-five minutes of their precious off-duty drinking time. They were not impressed. Superintendent Cluskey leaned over the dispenser as Ash pulled him his pint and said, "I hope you show more respect for the law and Mr Milligan in future, young Ashley. Otherwise there'll be another pillow-biting fairy on the unemployment blacklist."

Ash topped up the pint without batting an eyelid. Wordlessly he placed it on a dripmat and turned away. He busied himself changing an optic. In the corner of his eye he glimpsed the mirror again and saw how pale he looked. That policeman was just one rank away from chief super. Ash was genuinely uptight now. Bad enough that his demeanour made it obvious he was gay, it was something he just could not hide, but if Milligan ever figured out he dressed up... Gays were barely tolerated around here. As for a cross-dresser holding down a job in a place like this, he just would not have a chance.

Ash avoided Superintendent Cluskey by spending the rest of his shift at the far end of the counter. He did serve them once just to show there were no hard feelings. He pulled nineteen ounces of the finest beer into a pint glass that already contained an ounce of kinkiest spittle. As he served it reverentially to the new chief-to-be, he overheard a snippet of conversation between Cluskey and a great white shark who had joined them. Something about the birthrate in the outer suburbs. "They breed like rats," the politician said, echoing clearly the sentiments of the policemen around him.

It was not only the law and the politicians. The media had also swung to the right, as well as much of the general public. Crime levels were such that harsh measures were in the air. Not for the first time had Ash overheard the argument that strict birth control measures should be enforced in the more crowded parts of town, especially among refugees and asylum seekers. It was a notion that was gaining legitimacy, if some of the comments in the Contemplative Bar were anything to go by. Ash was not the first bartender in the world to be privy to the inner thoughts of judges and politicians, nor would he be the last.

Ash rode the midnight rail to Westown. The late ride was relatively hassle-free; there was only one unscheduled stop. The brakes screeched, the train lurched. Ash felt a barely perceptible bump as something flew out from under the wheels. Too dark for a sheep, too small for a horse, Ash recognised it as half of something. It rolled back off the embankment toward the track, its two legs and tail still thrashing the air. Ash could see the flailing, convulsing limbs. They were attached to a large lump of swollen red meat that pumped blood high and dark into the Dublin night. It was the hindquarters of a large dog, probably somebody's alsatian. The other half was doubtless tied to the line, its heart probably still beating beneath the train. He heard youngsters laughing. The railway guards soon chased them away.

The train stayed motionless for five minutes before proceeding slowly to the station. Somewhere at the back of the carriage a brick smacked off a window. Ash leaned back from the glass in case his window was hit. When the train pulled in he skipped off the end of the platform and made for the shortcut by the tracks. He knew better than to walk under streetlamps around here. At this hour gangs hung loose on corners, itching for passers-by. Penknives peeped out of pockets, knuckledusters stood rigid on fists, broken bottles waited patiently for a face to slash, syringes twiddled their thumbs waiting for someone to jab. In Westown everything that seeped into gutters during daytime came oozing back up at night.

Ash skipped past the sloe bushes and scampered up the embankment. He stood for a moment. Row upon row of uniformly terraced houses stretched endlessly before him. The colour of night was kind. The twinkling of stars made the scene look almost pretty, the way so many million rooftops crowded in on each other like that, sparkling in the starlight. Ash found himself wondering for the thousandth time what he was doing living in a dump like this with his boring sister Lesley and her dickhead husband, Brian. He was in the middle of thinking about it when something grated in the gravelly undergrowth. It moved too. Ash jumped with fright, then shook his head with relief. It was a sheep, as scrawny and scraggly as the tree it was tied to. Half-starved, half-ridden to death by the local eight year-olds, it stared up at him.

"Well, Brian?" he said, leaning toward the sheep's battered face. "Wondering where all the meadows have gone, eh Brian?"

The sheep bleated pathetically and scratched the earth. Ash straightened up and looked again at the terraced rows. Then he glanced down at the sheep. He thought of Brian sitting across from him at Sunday lunch, that pathetic little family ritual Lesley insisted they take part in. 'In honour of mam and dad', she said. Fuck mam and dad for dying so young; fuck them for leaving him with such a half-baked family. The sheep had Brian's face. No wonder Ash had to drop a tab every Sunday morning, and then another one as soon as his brother-in-law opened his mouth.

In the distance a dog barked. In one of the houses opposite, a baby cried. From somewhere nearby Ash heard a squeal of delight - or was it a scream of terror? "Goodnight, Brian," he said, running down the path to 97 Valhalla Drive.

* * *

"How was your trip home?" Lesley cornered him in the hallway.

"Not bad," he mumbled, "only two ambushes." It crossed his mind that she might have meant the pun in her greeting, but tonight she sounded more cheerful than cynical.

Ash was hungry. He brushed past her and made for the kitchen. She followed him and said, "I've good news, Ash."

He knew what it was before she said another word, but pretended not to have a clue. He stood at the micro with his hand on the dial, turned to her and said, "Yeah, what?"

"I'm pregnant." All of a sudden she took two steps across the kitchen floor and had him in her arms. She swung him around so hard his back hit the microwave door but she did not care. "I'm preggers!" she sang, twirling him around again and again in those big arms of hers.

"Take it easy, take it easy." He stopped her in mid-twirl and looked into her eyes. They were deep and dark like a turtle's. In them he saw happiness he had not known in her before. Her dream was finally on its way. "When did you find out?" he asked.

"At the clinic at seven o'clock this evening."

"Does Brian know yet?"

"No, he's on the night shift. He'll be home at three."

"So he finally managed to get it u-" Ash never finished his sentence. His sister punched his stomach so hard he doubled up in a crazy cocktail of mock surprise, real pain and genuine laughter.

Ash had his supper, dressed up and went out. He skipped around the edges of the estates. The cover of local knowledge, of shortcuts quick and dark, and his black greatcoat cloaked him from the gangs that preyed on those with less careful ways. Lesley's news had put him in the mood for having a good time. Amazing, his sister was finally up the pole. He never thought Brian had it in him. He did not want to be in the house when Brian came in off his shift. They were entitled to some privacy especially when a wife had such news for her husband. Ash felt light-headed, not just from the tab he dropped. He also felt guilty about leaving Lesley on her own, which he put down to feeling more protective of her now. He thought too of the proposed new birth-control laws. No way would they introduce retrospective abortion - they could never backdate it, never.

Within thirty minutes he was at the park. Most of the girls were there, scuffing high heels on the pavement, hanging around lamp-posts, leaning on car windows checking out clients. Ash wanted to tell Sylvia about his sister, and he did - even though Shirley was perched alongside her on the bench.

"I thought he couldn't get it up," said Sylvia.

"They used matchsticks for splints."

Sylvia screamed with laughter, even Shirley could not hide a smile. "But isn't he, what's his name, isn't he a bit of a dickhead?" said Sylvia.

"Brian? Yeah, but he's not the worst."

"He works as a security man at the chemical plant in Westown, doesn't he?" Shirley stood up and began straightening out her skirt. Ash could see what was coming. "Amazing how people will scrounge for a living when they're afraid to try more adventurous ways," she said in that chirpy voice of hers. She turned and waggled her prim bottom at a kerb-crawling merc. When it slowed to a halt she sauntered over to the driver.

"That bitch. I'll have her balls some day," said Ash.

"Don't let her annoy you, Ashley. It just gets to her that we do it for fun, that we're not on the game."

"It's not just that. She's getting at me for the day-job."

"You're paranoid," Sylvia said. "Mind you, she has a point. I don't know how you can serve drink to those bollixes. I must go in there again some time though, for the fun of it - don't worry, not when you're on duty! Do they still have that crazy sign on the empty TV bracket: 'Conan's - no TV's, not even for sport'?"

The smile was back on Ash's face now. Sylvia was always a laugh. She knew that Ash helped Lesley and Brian with the rent and that without him, his sister and brother-in-law would be on the street. But he was more than a lodger - he was family. Despite Sylvia's gentle chiding of his workplace he knew she understood that the money was good and that he needed it. As for Shirley's more adventurous ways, he had tried that too but in the unwashed creases of filthy strangers he had found only desperation and loneliness. As for the twisted, inverted street-snobbery of Shirley's attitude, she was welcome to the momentary attentions of the rich. Let her run the risk of diseases and abusive clients. As for Ash, the money in his handbag and a few thrills with Sylvia were enough for any night out. That and a few tabs, of course. Ash popped another one now and stared at a new girl standing on the far side of the road that bisected the park. Sylvia noticed her too. "Her name's Emma. Only seventeen. Pretty, isn't she?" she said.

Ash nodded in agreement.

Night sky grew black as tar on a dark, dark sea. Ash moved his head from side to side. The streetlights whizzed overhead like comets across the vault of heaven. The bench became a swaying hammock above the green, green grass. Sylvia became mother of all mothers, father of all fathers, lover of all lovers - and the sirens, the flashing blue lights, the screeching brakes, the shouting voices, were mere intruders at the edge of a universe serene and beautiful.

Not so to Sylvia, who had popped only one pill. "The cops!" she hissed, pulling Ash into the cover of bushes behind the bench. The jolt, the shock, the shuddering effect of cold earth, brought Ash down enough to realise what was happening and to focus, however fuzzily, however briefly, on it.

He saw Shirley and the girls. He saw them hair-pulled and crotch-kicked into cars and vans. Some screamed, others ran. Uniforms, dark and slick like oil running fast in the night, chased them down and beat them viciously. Ash felt their pain, their thuds and thumps, in a strange detached way as if it was happening in a film and he was crouching in some dark and thorny auditorium. It was a sad, moving film. He stared at scenes of sadness, his vision blurred from tears that rimmed his eyes. Unable to play the hero because of fear, because of drugs, he and Sylvia watched helplessly as the police brutalised their victims.

The last view Ash had of Shirley was of her being dragged by the hair into a wire-meshed cage-car. Her tight skirt was creased now and her lovely jacket all in a mess. Ash felt sorry even for her, but the terror was not yet over. Batons swooped through the air in slow-motion, heads crunched sideways under impact. That new seventeen year-old, Emma, was one of the last to be cornered. She had cowered behind a bush on the other side of the bench. Tiny and harmless as her adopted name, she crouched low but a thorn had caught her blouse and the branch whip-lashed against the leg of a policeman. He stared down at her, motionless. His face broke into a crooked smile, a familiar smile. Ash froze. It was Cluskey, the new chief-to-be, one of the officers he had sent on a wild goose chase the previous shift. The sneer was unmistakable. Twenty tabs would not make Ash forget it, never mind three.

The policeman stared down forever, a tower of strength in the strife-torn night. Little Emma petrified, a crumpled-up ball of innocence and fright. All her dreams torn, just like her brand new dress. Ash and Sylvia clung to each other, afraid to make a noise. Aeons passed. The giant policeman slapped his baton idly on the palm of his left hand. It made a fleshy repetitive sound. Then Cluskey put his hand into his pocket and called out, "Are they all rounded up, lads?"

"Yes, sir," cried a voice in the darkness.

From out of his pocket Cluskey took a rubber ring. He attached it to the top of his baton. All the while he smiled down at Emma. She in turn stared up with a face like bleached bone -

Ash could not get over the colour. Whatever it is about the strange silvery light that invades public parks at night, it sure makes people look white. Emma's pale face grew streaked now and her nose and mouth began to quiver and shake as Cluskey slowly unrolled the condom over the length of the baton. All the while the smile, all the while a whimper that grew ever louder, ever shriller. "No," she pleaded. "No!" Again that idle tickle of hard baton on soft hand. It sounded different now. Never was a baton so erect. Then the power-swing, the vicious arc, the crack of reinforced rubber on fragile skull. Once, twice, three times, four. Three of Cluskey's favourite sperm - hatred, fury, bigotry - spurted down the length of his shaft onto Emma's skull. They swam through her head into her brain and poisoned her. She was dead within seconds.

There came the sound of footsteps running, and a voice, "Sir! Sir!"

"Don't worry, son," said the super to the sergeant as he held up the blood-soaked condom in the moonlight. "We'll leave this dead pervert here as an example. It'll serve him right."

"You fucking bitch! You bitch!"

Ash was distraught. Sylvia was furious. He had tried not to tell her but in the end it just came out. "You served him. Him! How could you do that! How!"

They were down the docks now, miles from the park. Sylvia's fury was boundless and justified. Ash knew that. He replied, feebly, that work in the city was the only way out for him, and for Lesley and Brian.

"You fucking hypocrite! You serve him drink. You cow-tow to him - him and how many others like him!"

"It's only a job. It's-"

"Only a job? You fucking gobshite." Sylvia smeared what little mascara was left even further across her cheeks and spat in Ash's face. "You'll never get out of the gutter. None of us will.

Can't you see that? Go fuck yourself - don't ever come near me
again!"

She turned and was gone. Ash knew he had lost her forever.
From the chill night air he could pull no Houdini-like words to
entice her to change her mind. He could find no words at all, not
even the most prosaic. He tore off the thorn-shredded remnants
of his greatcoat and sat on the dock. Above him a crane-hook
creaked in the night. He sat there, Sylvia's spittle drying on his
face. He took one last look at his handbag. There were two tabs
in the zip pocket. Ash popped them both and flung the bag into
the tide. There was no more fun now, no more Sylvia, no more
anything.

Ash looked down at the river and saw Emma's face shivering and quaking with fear - perhaps it was a contortion brought
about by ripples. He saw Lesley twirling him around in her big
fat arms. Was the microwave door banjaxed, he wondered? He
pitied whatever mite she bore and the pathetic future that lay in
store for it. He saw Brian, the dickhead, working his ass off on
security duty at the chemical plant. Poor old Brian - proud
daddy, shit world. Ash saw Sylvia's bright eyes and kissy curls.
Then his tears mixed with her saliva and together fell into the
river. What a compound they made, potent drops of Ashen tears
and Sylvian saliva. When they hit the surface they reacted to the
water in a most peculiar way.

A salmon came from nowhere. It swam to the surface at the
dockside. A salmon in this river, in the year of our pollution two
thousand and something - Ash could not believe it. He reached
down but the dorsal fin flipped over and the fish was gone. Ash
remembered something about a salmon, something from his
schooldays. There was a fable: eat the salmon and possess infi-
nite wisdom. Ash longed to taste the salmon and gain from it the
knowledge, the wisdom, to know what to do. If only he could
reach down and catch it. The salmon appeared again. It stared
up at him invitingly. Ash reached down. He felt sure the salmon

would know. He stretched his arm out. Slowly he felt himself slipping over the edge. Suddenly the salmon leaped out of the water and jumped up at him. Its mouth hit him square on the lips and pushed him flat on his back on the dockside. Ash felt something fall heavily on his stomach and slither down his leg. He pushed himself up on his hands just in time to see a splash as a tail fin disappeared beneath the waves. He shook his head in amazement and licked his lips. There was no taste of salmon.

Ash sat at the table in 97 Valhalla Drive. Sunday lunch, Boringday lunch. Brian was talking about some football match, as usual. Ash was only half-listening. He stared out the back window at the embankment and remembered a sheep tied to a tree. He wondered if it was dead now. Probably. Lesley was also quite talkative today. Her scan had shown the baby to be developing nicely. There had been no problem healthwise in the four weeks since her pregnancy had been confirmed. The government had announced curbs on population growth, especially among non-nationals, in the outer suburbs. Lesley and Brian were relieved to hear they would not affect current pregnancies. Ash let his sister and her husband talk while he sipped wine. Brian flicked on the wall-vid. Lesley looked over and said, "It's a change to see you taking wine instead of tabs, Ash."

"Yeah, what's come over you? You haven't borrowed any clothes off Les lately, either."

"Brian!" Her husband was too busy tuning in the vid to notice her throwing up her eyes at the insensitive comment he had made.

"It's okay." Ash shared out the bottle of finest South African he had smuggled out of Conan's. Brian was too gormless to mean any harm. He was just talking about clothes, never intending such a remark to remind Ash of Sylvia.

The Euroleague match had already kicked off - Dublin against some team from Italy. Amazing how televised football had become the panacea to the masses, ruthlessly hyped yet still regarded by most people as some kind of sport. Ash was grateful that it would pre-occupy his brother-in-law for the next couple of hours.

A player threw himself feet-first at the ball, timing his touch to perfection. The ball shot out of play as a winger hurdled over the defender's outstretched leg and grabbed the corner flag with one hand as he went flying past the endline. Ash had never been this close to the wall-vid for a match before. It filled his whole vision. He had never seen a flagpole swing like a metronome on tabs before. Some analyst on the vid - there was always at least a pair of them constantly chattering - screamed that it was the best slider he had ever seen. They showed a replay of it. The corner flag swayed in slo-mo, the action cut to a throw-in and Ash lost interest in what the wall-vid showed him. He had called to Sylvia's flat two days after the park. She was dressed straight, afraid to be herself in case she broke the new Anti-Social Codes the government had introduced in the wake of Emma's death. The murder in the park had given them the excuse they needed. Cross-dressing was illegal now under emergency ASC's. A lot of other things were declared illegal as well. Sylvia blamed Ash for being part of the rotten system that had killed Emma and imprisoned their friends. Arguments about it being only a job did not convince her. "You're a fucking arsehole," she said, slamming the door in his face.

Brian jumped out of his seat screaming, groaning - a camera in the back of the net showed the ball thundering off the crossbar, the nearest Dublin had come to scoring. Ash could not figure who had made more noise: his brother-in-law or the fifty thousand people at the match. Brian sat back and Ash was soon lost in thought again. In Sylvia's eyes he saw himself reflected, and through her eyes he glimpsed what she saw him as: coward, wimp, hypocrite. Superintendent Cluskey came into Conan's four nights after the park. The bartender looked the same to him, and young Ashley continued to serve Conan's customers as if nothing had changed. But behind the sap-faced youth, under his long grey hair, nothing was ever going to be quite as it was. Ash sometimes looked around him as he polished glasses and filled pints. It saddened him when he saw the delightful decor, the soulful lighting, the subtle ambience. It was all a sham, as see-through as the tumbler in his hand. There was a time when the idea behind the Contemplative Bar was good, Ash knew that. But the lonely souls who had once sought a haven from the relentless progress of modernity had themselves been replaced by a clientele with no such romantic notions. Conan Milligan was not a bad man. He had not set out to deliberately build a talking shop for a repressive establishment. It just happened that way, in the same way that Ash just happened to be on his staff. Ash took another sip and looked up. A yellow card, followed by red, and a sky-blue Dub took the long lonely march to the tunnel.

Ash continued to serve Cluskey, to serve him obsequiously. The child within him could not resist devising a trick or two, like slipping a note in Cluskey's coat, a note that would say, "I saw what you did." Or a dripping-red condom on Cluskey's wiper-blade would be worth it for the look on the superintendent's face if someone walked into the bar to tell him what had been attached to his car. Ash smiled at such thoughts. Thoughts they remained. When he served Cluskey again he filled the pint with twenty ounces of finest beer and not a trace of spittle. Ash sighed. The ball flew toward the top corner but the keeper stretched full-length and tipped the ball around a post.

Lesley looked at her watch. "Time to put the kettle on for half-time," she said.

Time, yes. Time was important. The referee was looking at his watch. He blew the whistle. Lesley went to the kitchen to fetch the tea. Brian started to rabbit on about the match. Ash went to the front window of 97 Valhalla Drive and looked out.

Somewhere out there a river flowed. When Ash took all those tabs it would flow broad and narrow, brackish and crystal clear, sluggish and fast. It would be shallow and deep and choked with pollution and teeming with life. In it Ash would see the Sylvia he had lost. In it he would see Cluskey the child-killer, Cluskey the witty barstool raconteur, and no doubt Cluskey the charming family man too. Yes, he would be there. Everyone was there.

"I'm just going out for a walk," said Ash before slipping out the front door and popping a bagful of tabs. He skipped around the edges of the estates. The cover of local knowledge and his black greatcoat cloaked him as he made his way to the river.

Evening was closing in. Ash stood on the parapet of the bridge, the parapet of life itself. Tonight the starlight would shine down brightly on all those millions of rooftops. It would make them look almost pretty, the way they crowded in on each other. Tonight there would be that extra twinkle, the colour of night would be kind, and Dublin would be a better, cleaner place. Ash looked out over the city to where Lesley and Brian might play with their child in the streets, to where the sheep might return to the meadow and the salmon might leap in the river. Yes, someday he would dress up again. So too would Sylvia and together they would dance in the park beneath shining stars, skipping lightly over the grass like wingers soaring over a sliding tackle.

Walk With Me

"You workin' for Al Khali?" shouted the ferryman over the putt-putt of an outboard in need of a service.

His passenger nodded and looked out over the sea. At least the crossing was calm, Bates was thankful for that considering the skinful of drink he'd had the night before.

"He's crazy," said the sea-dog, "crazy as a coot, tryin' to build a hotel and leisure complex on an uninhabited island. More money than sense, if you ask me."

Bates smiled. He didn't know how much wealthy Kuwaiti businessmen were worth and he didn't care. They paid a lot for dowsing jobs, though.

"Reckon there's water there?" The ferryman pointed beyond a flock of cartwheeling skuas to the rocky shore.

"I hope so," said Bates, more interested in a looming cliff.

"Pity sheep don't dig wells," said the ferryman. "So many

sheep on that island it's a leisure centre already, eh?" He winked and laughed so loud it matched the outboard.

Bates sighed inwardly. Swimming would have been better than putting up with this old salt's jackhammer humour, but the cove was near - just behind the north-facing headland beyond the cliff. Peculiar thing about the cliff; it too looked north, but unlike the headland, its rocky slopes were in shade. Bates glanced from cliff to headland then back again. Definitely all shadow. A trick of the light, perhaps. Before he could figure it out, the sea-dog barked something about Argyle men wearing kilts because highland sheep could hear a zip going down at two hundred metres.

This time Bates sighed out loud but the ferryman never shut up, not even after his passenger had lugged his gear over the side and jumped ashore. The sea-dog leaned on his spluttering outboard, roaring something about peregrines and promising to be back by two o'clock.

Bates waved perfunctorily and glanced at his watch. Five hours ought to be enough. Balancing like a tightrope walker, he picked his way over a beach brimming with large stones, smooth and round as bowling balls. He clambered up a rocky slope. Arms stiff from balancing his load, he gratefully dropped his equipment on top of a grassy knoll. Hands on hips, he surveyed the scene before him.

The island was small: four kilometres by two. One glance told Bates the Kuwaiti was right about one thing: gently undulating contours would make a fine golf course. To the south, long sandy beaches, as white as any Bates had seen. Virgin white to match a sunseeker's dream. But this was no glossy brochure; this was Scotland. He looked up at a kind sky and wondered if Al Khali had ever seen the island in Atlantic weather. He uncapped his rollerful of charts and unfurled a map.

The proposed hotel and leisure centre lay to the south near the white beaches. The clubhouse complex was earmarked for the east, up from the cove where he had landed. A water source did exist, a small spring, but it was on the western tip of the island, suitable only for supplying the sheep. Al Khali's surveyors had earmarked several sites, hoping to reach the water-table with boreholes.

Bates was ready to dowse when he saw what was on the northern side.

Up from the island summit, three hundred metres above the sea, a standing stone stood tall and erect against the northern sky. Bates consulted his chart. According to ordnance details, it marked an ancient burial site. He rolled up his chart, all the while staring at the stone. *Neolithic*, the map said. It leaned at an angle now, reminding him of a crocodile's upper jaw opened wide to catch butterflies. The breeze strengthened. He shivered though it was May, stuffed the chart into his brown snow-jacket, and unpacked the tools of his trade.

His fingers worked for him, without him. Forked hazel dipped and jerked as he walked over tight, sheep-cropped grass. His hands took on a life of their own. Tremors and twitches conveyed the pattern of energy-lines he needed to know. A preliminary dowse over the map had made things easy. By 11am results were promising: water accessible south and east. Bates paused for a hot slug of soup from his flask. He sat on a rocky outcrop. The breeze was consistent. The sky had lost its blue, darkening the rising swell. Bates did not notice the gathering of white horses. His eyes were drawn to the lone sentry on the hill, stark now against distant grey sky.

Out of the clouds something swooped. Large and silent, its flailing wingspan cast no shadow. Bates was alerted only by the flapping of its wings. It was almost on him. He ducked, startled. It flew past, squawking a loud screeching cackle that did Bates no good at all. Damn peregrine.

He set to work again. With gently twirling pendulum, forked

hazel and willow, and a pair of L-shaped rods to provide that extra dimension - in and out as well as up and down - he found not only the water's location but also its depth, rate of flow, and that it was suitable for drinking. He also divined something else. What it was he did not know. The force-lines were not right, not splaying in the usual way like the branches of a tree. Instead, they pointed in one direction: to the island summit. Bates looked again at the standing stone. Behind it, the cliff he had seen earlier, the cliff that refused light. He glanced at his chart. Two lines of markers pointed to the northern side of the island. He walked east, his curiosity equal to the hunger pangs gnawing at his gullet. He checked his watch. Noon. The bulk of the work done, requisite sites pinpointed for Al Khali, he could now devote a couple of hours to the intriguing pattern unfolding before him. But his hangover came first, nothing that a good lunch wouldn't cure.

He came to a hollow just above the shore on the eastern side. A sheltered spot, ideal for lunch. He had not been the first to think that. In the hollow were traces of a campfire, a couple of weeks old by the look of it. Realising who had made that fire, Bates felt a sudden chill. He sat down. Unwrapping his salad roll, he recalled what a local had told him in the mainland pub the previous night. There had been a murder on the island less than a fortnight previously. An Australian girl, travelling solo, had come to spend a few days studying birds. There had been no sign of her when the ferryman returned to take her back to the mainland. A police search unearthed no clues. Her tent had been left undisturbed. Everything was in its proper place, but they could not find her. Bates shifted uneasily in the knowledge that he was sitting where she had pitched her last, fateful camp.

He played the salad roll like a harmonica, nibbling the crust down one side, then the other. How, he had asked the local, did they know she was murdered if they never found the body? The highlander cleared his throat, called for a pair of malts, and told him of a barbed wire fence some metres back from the edge of the cliff. To keep the sheep from falling off, he had said. That was where she fell, or jumped, or was pushed. No one was sure which. A strip of human flesh, ten inches long, the length of the local's forearm, was found hanging from one of the barbs. Lab tests showed it to be only days old, from the thigh of a young woman.

Edges chewed off, Bates tackled the roll head-on. He bit off great chunks, spitting tomato pips at the little patch of darkened turf, almost reclaimed now by new grass. He squinted at the distant standing stone. Beyond it, the fence - a good few metres back from the cliff-edge. No way could she have fallen off and rolled over into the sea. Imagine the terror in her mind, the local had said, to make her tear off ten inches of her own flesh in a bid to get away from whoever, or whatever, was after her. It didn't bear thinking about. Bates found himself thinking of his girlfriend, Melanie, and the life they had started together in London. That Australian girl was somebody's Melanie. He brushed the crumbs from his jacket and trouser legs. He lifted the edge of his chart and began sliding it between his teeth like a makeshift toothpick. Then it dawned on him.

Eagerly, he flattened his chart on the grass. He pulled one of the L-shaped rods from his bag and used it as a ruler to draw a line from the water sources in the south to the northern shore, then repeated the exercise with the eastern sources. He glanced at the distant standing stone and checked his chart again. Both lines intersected at the spot marked *monument*. Bates knew that standing stones were often centred on force-lines, but he had never known vibrations as strong as this from a source almost two kilometres away.

He stuffed his chart into the side pocket of his jacket. Stepping gingerly across the spongy turf, he made his way to the centre of the island where he took out his favourite rod of forked hazel. He pointed its single end to the north. The rod jerked so hard it nearly snapped in his hands. It was a force so powerful the hazel rasped against the fulcrum of his fists. He turned quickly to one side. The power in the rod died. He took out the chart, marked the spot, and whistled. A find like this would cement his reputation as a dowser of great repute. It might make him famous and bring in enough money to buy that apartment Melanie wanted. Whatever the source of the energy-lines, he determined to track it down and identify it.

He walked straight for the standing stone, forked hazel hanging loosely by his side. The nearer he came to it, the more the rod began to writhe like a wet fish in his fingers. He stood at the bottom of the hill leading to the stone, hazel twisting and turning in his hand. Holding the forked end firmly, he pointed north. The stick sprang back, its single end nearly tearing itself off the fork, the fork-end almost wrenching the skin off his hand. The rod catapulted back through the air, landing ten metres away. Bates turned around, astonished at such a reaction.

With the drink-induced cobwebs in his head well and truly blown away, he bent to pick up the rod. This was incredible. He looked around and saw the tide, racing now. He saw the threatening sky, and the stone. All his life he had waited for a force like this, but his excitement was tempered by the memory of what the highlander had said the previous night. This was a strange place. Superstition attached itself to it with all the stubborn strength of limpets on the rocks below. Legend had it that people were once sacrificed from the cliff-top. Lots of shipwrecks, too. The island had never been inhabited in recent times, not even by crofters, though a family had tried to live here centuries before. A wild family - savages, by all accounts. One of them went crazy and killed the others. Cooked their bodies, and ate them, too.

Bates grimaced at such local history and looked out to sea. The wind was picking up, making the water choppier. The cliff-top could be a dangerous place in squally conditions. He held the rod out once again, gripping it tightly for fear it might break. It didn't, but he needed both hands. When he turned away from the stone, the rod went limp. Amazed, Bates considered abandoning his attempt to dowse the cliff-top because of the weather, but felt compelled to go on. No one had ever divined a force so strong, so sinister. He forced himself to think of Melanie. If only she were here they could walk together, each holding the rod two-handed. *Walk with me, Melanie*, he whispered, guiding the rod until it pointed at the stone. It jerked convulsively.

Fighting the rod, holding on tight, Bates neared the spot where it had earlier flown from his hand. As soon as he reached the foot of the hill, the hazel jerked so violently he couldn't control it. This time the wind, the force - whichever it was - flung the rod back thirty metres.

Bates looked at the mainland, to where a motorboat breached the marching lines of riotous waves, its red hull tossing from side to side and up and down. He watched it cut through the tidal channel. It was the old sea-dog coming to take him away from the island. He looked out over the sea. Flocks of gulls and guillemots swirled and dipped in salt-strewn air. White horses galloped into the bay. Breakers dashed themselves to death on the rocks below.

He stood at the foot of the hill, rummaging through his bag of gear, filling his pockets with pendulum, willow, and L-shaped rods as back-up in case the hazel broke. Hands held out, he stepped forward.

Up the hill he plodded, rod gyrating in his hand, an irresistible force warping it up and back alarmingly. Fighting hard to keep wrists and wood from breaking, Bates walked head down into a gale that swept up and over the shadowy cliff. Fifty metres from the stone, the rod had bent so much it almost touched his nose. Then it snapped. The broken twig tried hard to take his eye out as it flew past, grazing his cheek. Startled to find hazel-drawn blood trickling down his face, he glanced up. The stone seemed larger now, bigger than before. It didn't lean at an angle any more. It stood erect against the thunderous sky. He thought that might have something to do with the angle he was viewing it from.

He took the willow out of his pocket. The wind whipped up a good force ten. He stepped forward. Willow-wood imitated hazel as it jerked up fiercely. On top of the hill now, Bates circled slowly around the stone, edging ever closer to it. In its struggle to break free, the willow wrenched itself from his grip and shot past his left ear. Struggling to keep a foothold in the wind, he looked at the weals on his hands made red and swollen by the will to divine.

The stone towered over him; dark, looming, brooding. Gulls cackled overhead. Peregrines swooped again. The side of his jacket bulged - the pendulum was trying to escape. He opened his pocket. Out it jumped, making for the ground, rolling - bouncing - along grass, through mounds of sheep shit, to the fence. Gathering momentum, it raced beneath the lowest barbed wire out over the cliff to the rocks below. Stunned, Bates fought the wind, and his better judgement, which told him to escape, to run, to hide. But he had to find out. He had to keep going.

Birds wheeled everywhere. Stormy petrels in his mind, Bates thought one last time of Melanie. He pointed the remaining rods, the L-shaped ones, at the monument. Whatever dynamics lurked within the stone went to work, splaying the rods in opposite directions until Bates stood like a man crucified. The wind took him then, lifting him, ramming him into the fence. His back crashed into a post. Barbs tore at his jacket, his trousers, his skin. The fencepost cracked from the battering ram of his body, and collapsed. Trailing strips of cloth and flesh, he was blown over the grass. Then he ran out of grass. The last thing he saw was a standing stone somersaulting. The whole world went upside down. He tumbled upside down, and the rocks came up to greet him.

The island was alone again. Skuas and peregrines cartwheeled overhead, and the stone leaned at an angle once more, like a crocodile's jaw opened wide.

Flying Kites

Rekdar shut down alto-mode and waited for the hover to settle gently on a bed of what looked like moss, except for the colour. Scanners had analysed it as a lichenous growth covering the entire planet. Its brittle pink tentacles, no more than three centimetres deep, welcomed the hover with a soft, scrunchy embrace.

"Systems off," said Rekdar. When the dull whirr of the hover wound itself down, he ordered GEM to patch him through to Control. He reported his exact co-ordinates, switched off GEM, and requested permission to begin phase two alone.

"Negative," replied Control. "GEM required for environmental analysis."

"Control," said Rekdar. "You also want to monitor my feelings and reactions to these new surroundings, correct?"

"Correct."

"My reactions will be more authentic if I EVA alone."

"Request denied. Environment uncharted. EVA potentially hazardous."

Rekdar paused momentarily before flicking GEM back on. He hadn't expected that ploy to work, but anything was worth a try to switch off the infernal scanalytic unit they had attached to the side of his face.

Rekdar's boots bit into pink lichen with the satisfying crunch of footfalls in snow. The ground beneath was hard and also pink. GEM quickly confirmed it was the same all over. The survey team's mobile units had EVA'd simultaneously at nine different locations and were all busily scanning the surface. GEM now had a planet-wide profile, and was not long in completing its study.

"Phase three - confirm individual assignments," said GEM.

"Confirm VK Recon." Rekdar, aware that the GEM on his face was now operating independently of Control, stepped toward the ridge overlooking his VK assignment.

Rekdar had drawn the best hand when Control dealt from its pack of chosen sites. The eight other team members were given mountains, craters, plains, rivers. Rekdar had drawn the ace: VK - Valley of the Kites. GEM called them Tetrahedral Pretensiled Objects: TPO's for short. Rekdar needed just a glance to christen them kites - a term that quickly stuck with his co-surveyors. GEM was reluctant to use that name - because they were not kites - and only grudgingly accepted the acronym VK for Rekdar's assignment.

Rekdar stood on the ridge. Everything on the planet varied from pinkish white to light red. There was one exception - the kites were yellow; hanging in the air like a freeze frame from a Chinese festival, or a snapshot of a beach in summer. Not vidshots, stills. The kites did not move. No flicking, no dabbing, no thrusting; no trick-of-the-loop, no tangled tails; no riding thermals, no eddying in currents because there were no currents - at least none that Rekdar could feel on his face.

One last look at the hover, one last check of the pulse gun attached to his belt, and Rekdar descended into the valley. He consoled himself with the thought that the human element was still needed in surveying: VK was a steep-walled box-canyon and no droid could match his climbing skills as he picked his way down an outcrop of pink rock; no flyer could manoeuvre where kites hung like barrage balloons in the sky.

Rekdar realised it was not luck, or fate, that dealt him that winning hand. It was logic - the cold logic of Control. Pick the best climber, also the most rebellious, give him the most dangerous EVA. If he doesn't come out alive, so what? They're all expendable, surveyors. All that mattered was the knowledge recorded by GEM. That's all that mattered to machines: knowledge, logic, data. It's why they monitored human feelings and emotions, to try to understand - to measure, to rationalise - the vagaries of the human mind, or heart, or whatever it was that made humans so truculent, so prone to error, so untrustworthy.

But machines were borne of humanity's greed. Now they controlled star systems and beyond; pillaging planets, killing off species - the ultimate humanity without humanity, pursuing history's greatest goal: conquest. With the takeover of machines came human enslavement and the manipulation of human consciousness. Like surveyors, all humans were expendable now; their hearts and minds rationalised into a slavish acceptance. Only occasionally did a spark of independence, of imagination, of rebellion, flicker - in men like Rekdar.

The rocky mountainside changed into a sharply inclined bed of scree. Arms out to maintain balance, Rekdar set off mini avalanches as he scurried down. Above him, between yellow kites and pink, rocky walls, he saw distant sky. It too had a reddish hue. Control was up there somewhere - in 500K orbit so it could see an entire hemisphere, except the valley floor beneath the kites.

Rekdar looked up at kite-heads floating like diamonds in the sky. They trailed twenty metres above the ground, twice a man's length in size, identical in colour and shape - no doubt the GEM-eye on his face had calculated their specifications by now. Rekdar's uncovered eye followed a yellow stem to the ground. Control had speculated that the kites were most likely plants, though their stems broadened as they grew. Botany was never Rekdar's strong suit, but he knew stems weren't normally like this. The stem where he stood was the width of a man's palm; the diameter of a well-fed thigh as it entered the kite. Wrinkly and bristled, it reminded him of an elongated mammoth trunk in shape and texture. He reached to caress the stem.

"Do not touch," snapped GEM. "VK must be mapped and assessed before TPO samples can be taken. All other action con-travenes assignment directive."

Rekdar bit his lip. GEM was fond of giving orders. Control had rigged him, it, both of them up as an experiment in neural-artificial co-operation - for their mutual benefit, as Control called it. For Control's benefit, as Rekdar called it. What he wouldn't give to unhook this state-of-the-art pain-in-the-butt from his face. Rekdar let his hand hover for more than a second near the kite's tiny bristles. GEM would never read such delays as defiance, same as it could never fathom that human curiosity sometimes outweighed strict scientific procedure. Bark samples, sap analysis, root investigation, would have to wait. Rekdar straightened his back and looked up. He thought the kite-head shifted slightly. Perhaps a breeze had picked up overhead.

Kites did not grow in neat rows, but sprouted at random along the valley floor. From its stationary orbit Control had counted 298 of them. No mathematical pattern was discernible, at least not to Rekdar's eye. Control had calculated a mean of eight metres between each kite-head. Rekdar turned his head slowly through one-eighty degrees as he walked along, so that GEM could compile a thorough profile of their surroundings.

Soon they came to the other end of the valley. Recording done, Rekdar turned around. An amazing sight stretched out all around. Pink terrain, yellow plants; a slow, slow haze caressed the landscape like a pink cloud coming from somewhere hidden, going to some place unknown. The quality of light was strange. Yellow kites diffused the pink sunlight, magically mellowing it into a heady mixture, like vapourised alcohol. Rekdar drank it in. He felt like a child in a brightly painted wonderland - the nearest he had ever been to a landscape wild and free of machines. He looked at the compelling sight above him. Beyond the yellow stems, kite-heads hung motionless as orchids in windless sunset. Rekdar felt as miniscule as an insect in a glori-ous flowerbed, and as insignificant. An explorer at one with a fabulous, uncharted world. He was at peace and yet oddly agi-tated. His heart pounded; he could feel its beat and hear it too. He stood on the brink of discovery, on the edge of emotion. GEM brought him back to reality with a jolt. "Emotional reaction monitored," it said. "Begin phase four."

Rekdar knelt before a kite-stem, scalpel ready. A shadow caught his eye. He looked up. Nothing moved. Holding the stem with his free hand, he steadied himself to take a sample. Incision an instant away, a millimetre away, he blinked, the stem blinked - or moved. Maybe it didn't, maybe it was him. Whatever it was, his red suit felt suddenly hot. He wiped his brow, scalpelled hand nearly ripping his forehead but he didn't notice.

Blade on bark. A slit: one centimetre, three, six - should be no more than five. Eight, nine - angling down, going out. Ten - out. Out because the stem was rising from the ground. Rekdar instinctively jumped back, kite-tail airbrushing his face as it swished past. Holding himself off the ground on his palms, he was instantly aware of three things; the wounded kite ascending to the sky; a frenetic popping noise all around; and GEM barking, "Rotate vision. Rotate vision."

Rekdar swivelled his head from side to side and up and down. The GEM-eye took it all in. So did Rekdar. Now he was aware of something else: terror. The popping was caused by hundreds of kite-tails escaping from the ground. They were all airborne, slowly ascending from the valley floor like missiles at Armageddon. Rekdar was ideally positioned to see them: his back on the ground now, his seeing eye mesmerised by the scene unfolding before him. The kites were in no hurry. Like slow-motion arrows converging on some lofty target, they arced lazily into the air, all headed for an invisible meeting-point high above the centre of the valley. Their movement was poetic, graceful, precise - too precise.

Rekdar reached the same conclusion as GEM and was on his feet before his facial unit instructed him to find shelter. He scarpered across the flat valley floor; so many tail-holes ready to break his ankle he couldn't risk glancing up, but GEM could see hundreds of kites spiralling like hawks. Rekdar was within six or seven seconds of a crevice in the valley-wall when GEM said, "TPO's attacking, TPO's attacking."

No one ever raised pink dust like Rekdar. The side of the valley was five seconds away when GEM said, "TPO's attacking. Seconds to impact: 3.8."

It took GEM more than two seconds to say that, which gave Rekdar time. Just. He sensed a shadow on his back, a great onrush of air on the hairs of his neck. He dived into the crevice as something large and yellow rushed past, followed by another and another. The fourth kite did not pull back in time. It crashed into the crevice. Luckily for Rekdar, it came at an angle, impacting into the rockface just inside the opening. An explosion of yellow liquid and bits of solid matter blew Rekdar further in. A quick look down and he saw not all the bits were yellow; some were pink - the kite had damaged the rockface. He was aware of other kite-heads whizzing past but mostly he was aware of the need to pull himself in as far as he could.

Two more kites crashed into the opening, again showering Rekdar with yellow blood, yellow flesh, and little bits of pink rock. By now he had wedged himself in at the deepest point of the crevice. Through a slit-like fissure in the rock he could see a slice of valley and kite-laden sky. The entrance through which he had come was around the corner from him. It was long and narrow, too narrow for kites. Another one hit, dislodging a large pink slate from above. Rekdar had seen enough to know what the kites were up to. "Give me all the data you can muster," he barked at GEM, "then get me Control."

Another explosion muffled his words, but GEM had heard. "Kites coming in at 57 degrees, 200K. 158 have veered away, 7 have impacted." Another one hit the rockface. "Control already contacted and aware of situation."

"Control," snapped Rekdar, "back-up needed. Confirm."

"Confirm back-up. ETA twenty min-" The voice from space was lost in a loud explosion that blew bits of rock everywhere.

Rekdar looked through a haze of pink dust at the crevice opening. It was wider. Another kite impacted, spewing great yellow blobs all over Rekdar. His voice rose perceptibly, not just to make himself heard. GEM responded with a damage report on the impact of kites on rockface: "Current rate of assault will widen crevice sufficiently to admit direct attack in less than six minutes."

Rekdar said nothing. Two more explosions rocked his hiding place. Then the pounding ceased. No more yellow shadows whizzed past. He strained his neck to look out. Through the narrow slit he could see a thin slice of pink valley and reddish sky. He dared not risk crawling past yellow-pink debris for a better view through the main opening. Control could see it all from its vantage point in space, and through the GEM-eye Rekdar could see it too.

Kites spiralled again like a huge catherine wheel - or a butcher's rotating blade. Their speed had slowed considerably. GEM confirmed that there were 271 of them, 27 having sacrificed themselves on the valley-wall. GEM soon detected an increase in speed and said, "Configuration changing. TPO's attacking."

Rekdar thought the pitch of GEM's voice was higher but he didn't have time to dwell on it. "Control!" he roared. "You've got to get here sooner. Repeat: you've got to-"

His voice was drowned by the horrendous impact of a kite. Coming in almost straight, it crashed into the crevice. Rekdar braced himself as the rockface shook. It shook again as another kite committed suicide, and another and another. Rekdar could barely hear Control's voice above the explosions. It told him back-up was sixteen minutes distant. GEM confirmed that the break-up of the opening in the rockface was a mere three minutes away.

"Any way we can signal peaceful intentions to the kites?" asked Rekdar above the surrounding noise.

"Negative," said GEM. "TPO's are impacting at random. There's no pattern to their attack. They-"

"What do you mean no pattern? Their intention seems obvious. They group, regroup, attack in formation. That's pattern en-" Rekdar's voice was lost in the din of another strike.

"Their behaviour is unprecedented," said GEM. "They do not group and regroup. They maintain the same formation, constantly spiralling. To attack, the spiral turns toward you; to pull back, the spiral turns away. There is no mathematical pattern to their method. Most of them are pulling away at the moment of impact. So are the others, but not in time."

"But then-" Rekdar shouted to make himself heard as the rockface shuddered, "-you mean they're not intending to hit the crevice?"

"Correct. They come in and veer away. Some don't veer in time."

"Show me," barked Rekdar.

Through the GEM-eye Rekdar saw Control's eye-in-the-sky view of the attacking kites. Sure enough, they were like flyers veering to avoid a cliff. Some reacted in time, others did not. Rekdar was suddenly aware that all was quiet again.

"Second wave over," said GEM. "TPO's turning toward us."

"Status?" asked Rekdar.

"215 remaining. Crevice opening now 68% of width required for direct entry."

Rekdar looked at his pulse gun. If there was no way of dissuading the kites from their attack, he had a way of dealing with them. At least, that's what he thought until GEM reminded him that his pulser held fifty charges. Even if his attrition rate was a 100%, and if the same proportion of kites self-destructed as before, he would only achieve a slight delay in the widening of the entrance, not enough until back-up came. In the end, as another assault began, his only hope was that his pulser might scare them off.

He braced his back against the rock, took aim through the slit-like fissure, and cut loose with half a dozen pulses. None found a target. Hard to line up a shot against kites looping in at 200K, not to mention taking steady aim through clouds of exploding rock and kite flesh, and an opening that vibrated whenever a kite hit home. The seventh pulse zapped a kite-head to bits, but the others kept coming relentlessly. Rekdar fired off thirty pulses for a meagre gain of five before GEM persuaded him that he was wasting his time.

The enemy spiralled like angels of death overhead. Sweat-soaked, covered in pink dust and bits of yellow mucus, Rekdar breathed hard. His training told him to ask GEM for a status report. His head told him the mathematics was against him. GEM confirmed what he already knew: too many kites, not enough time; the mothership didn't have the weaponry to tackle the enemy from 500K; Rekdar didn't have the weaponry to deal with them on the planet's surface. Billions of dollars worth of computer wizardry, the finest artificial intelligence in the universe, directly implanted into the side of his face, and it was telling him it was all over now. To hell with artificial intelligence if it was unable to tell him anything he did not already know. Anger grew in him like an ugly, giant tumour - anger at them wiring him up like this, anger at the kites, anger at Control, anger at...

"Emotion too negative, repeat, too-"

"Shut the fuck up!" barked Rekdar. "You put me here, you get me out. Surely your billion-dollar brain can analyse a way out of this?"

"Negative," replied GEM. "Impossible to ascertain which is the TPO you cut with your scalpel, or to ascertain if one of them has leadership qualities, or if herd instinct has taken over. TPO's totally unlike previously known life forms. Danger. Fourth attack wave commencing."

Through the GEM-eye Rekdar saw their battle configuration turn from stand-off to assault. No Ferris Wheel in a funpark, this. Like the blades of a circular saw, the spiralling kites turned until once again they were attacking the rockface.

The first impact almost disrupted Rekdar's train of thought. Something GEM said had set him thinking about herd instinct. Maybe it was that the valley-wall was a cliff, and the kites had a lemming-like attitude to death, but there was more to it than that. Another explosion: a gaping hole where once there was a narrow slit. Rekdar crouched into the rock as if it might cradle him. It was not so much instinct, it was what GEM had said . about the first kite - the one wounded by the scalpel.

"GEM! Can you track the first kite? The one I tried to take the sample from?"

"Negative. Impossible to ascertain where the spiral starts and ends."

Rekdar sighed and put his hands to his head as the rock shuddered from another impact. His brain shifted a gear as the dust cloud settled. "GEM!" he said. "Control! You've been recording all this from orbit, yes?"

"Correct," said Control.

"Then run the recording from the start, at speed until you catch up with present time. That way you'll spot the first kite, which may be their leader."

"Clarify."

"For Chrissake I haven't got time! They'll break through in a minute. Shouldn't take more than a second to scan the recording at high speed. Go back to the moment the first kite took off. That's the one I cut. Fast-forward 'til it catches up with itself!"

For an instant there was no reply. Rekdar was terrified he hadn't explained himself properly and was about to explain again when another explosion rammed the words down his throat. A great pink chunk of rock flew past his nose and crashed into the wall beside him, showering him with shard-like fragments. He was about to roar at Control again when GEM said, "Request granted. Observe."

The GEM-eye on Rekdar's head showed a split-screen image: on the left a man with a blade stooped to take a bark sample; on the right were deadly, wheeling kites bent on destroying his lair. The left side speeded up. The man jumped back, the kite took off followed by another and another. GEM coloured the lead kite bright red. It moved now not in slo-mo but fast. Very fast. Soon all the kites spiralled quickly before zooming in for the kill, wounded kite in the lead. Within seconds the attack was over. They spiralled and attacked again, red kite in front once more. GEM fast-forwarded the second assault, and the third and the fourth, until it matched the other image. Both in synch, GEM transferred the colour red to a kite rotating on the right.

Rekdar held his breath. If the kites were as primitive as GEM suggested, it was possible they were triggered by a base instinct in the wounded kite - a collective consciousness, a follow-the-leader reaction - which may have been brought on by Rekdar's scalpel. If that was so there was a chance. A small chance.

He moulded himself to the rock behind him. A new wave bore down, red kite to the fore. He fired a pulseful but the leader pulled away at the last moment, followed by the second and third. The next kite crashed into the opening, jarring Rekdar, terrifying him with the amount of rock it dislodged.

The unwinding spiral unleashed occasional hits, widening Rekdar's hiding place, shortening his life. GEM tracked the lead kite re-entering the wheel of circular death. More hits. More flying debris. Hard to concentrate with so much noise, so much fear; a hole so gaping each passing kite cast an ominous shadow on Rekdar's feet. He shuddered at the thought that soon more than shadows would pummel his pink flesh into pink rock. GEM alerted him that the lead kite was coming in again. He aimed through the narrow slit, desperately afraid of hitting the rock either side and bringing death down upon himself. He fired off pulses at that other death, that other fear, looming into his sights.

A pulse knocked the kite sideways. It veered left and crashed into the rockface. Shockwaves thundered through the rock, through Rekdar. Then more shockwaves, and more. One look through the GEM-eye told him why the shockwaves were unceasing. Kites were all kamikaze now; following their leader's flight path, throwing themselves one after the other at that same spot of pink rock, yellow now from mass suicide.

When the last kite had killed itself, Rekdar uncowered himself from his cleft in the wall. Out he went through blobs of kite flesh to the valley floor. There he saw where the kites had followed their leader's example. A great circle of yellow, tinged gold now by pink rock. Beneath it, gold-yellow flesh dripped onto a pile of kite-tails that had fallen to the ground. Rekdar gazed at them, awe-struck. GEM said, "Back-up: ETA four minutes thirty-two."

Rekdar slowly shook his head. Death had come close, so close. He stared at a rockface that was now the tombstone of 298 creatures. That gold-yellow circle of blood, sap, whatever it was, an epitaph to a mass-grave, the grave of an entire species. With a sickening sense of hopelessness and revulsion, Rekdar realised that he had wiped out the only colony of kites on the planet. He, Rekdar, had single-handedly destroyed them all. It did not matter how primitive they were. That they were hardly worth analysing, never mind preserving, was not important. His thoughts were interrupted by Control.

"Congratulations, Rekdar. You were right to assume TPO's followed a collective strategy. How did you reach this conclusion before GEM?"

Rekdar shrugged. "Human intuition," he smiled ruefully.

"Do you wish to have GEM disconnected forthwith?" asked an uncompromising Control.

Rekdar thought for a moment. A whole species had been destroyed to protect one man. Rekdar knew why. Humanity had created machines and now machines had turned Rekdar into a new machine-man. Somewhere in his mind he realised that this, the destruction of species, was humankind's ultimate legacy. He also knew that if this was so then humanity itself was at an end.

Rekdar took a deep breath. Walking slowly to the centre of the valley, pulse gun loose by his side, he stepped carefully between the tail-holes of creatures now extinct.

"Immediate reply requested," said Control.

Rekdar kept walking.

"Repeat. Do you wish to have GEM disconnected forthwith? Reply immediately."

Rekdar glanced up. "No," he said. "I never would have defeated the TPO's without GEM, and GEM never would have made it without me."

"Information assimilated," said Control, "and concurred. Your status will remain unchanged."

Rekdar stood at the valley centre. He looked up again. The GEM-eye instantly magnified, bringing the back-up mission into view. Rekdar took one look at the approaching craft. As his vision reverted to normal, he patted the metallic side of his face. His caressing hand betrayed its gentleness and became the vengeful weapon of all his pent-up rage.

Rekdar grabbed GEM and wrenched it from his face. With it came various bits and pieces: mainly artificial protein and neurone tubing, but also human meat. Lots of it. Skin, flesh, membranes, sinews, stretched and snapped; blood spurted from his head like a sideways geyser. He doubled up, his brain searing from the agonizing cry of torn nerve-ends. For an instant he was down on his haunches rocking in pain, the GEM in his hand dripping blood and viscous matter onto the valley floor.

With a great roar Rekdar sprang to his feet and flung GEM at the back-up craft. Up it went, twisting and turning, tumbling over and over. It glistened once in the pink light before disintegrating into a thousand pieces as Rekdar blasted it with his pulser. Only four pulses left, and only one non-zoom, real-time eye to see with. It was enough to see the back-up ship and with his mind's eye Rekdar saw Control. That was all he needed to keep him upright long enough for the last of his puny pulses to glance off the incoming fuselage. Then he fell to his knees screaming in pain, his spirit extinguished only by the final beat of his heart.

SOMETHING SMALL

Grub-kicking a pile of fallen leaves was not the most feminine thing for a nurse to do, but it was my way of announcing to the world that I was back, healthy as ever. A wind-devil caught the leaves and spiralled them back against the wall. Fewer leaves were scattered on the far side of the road, which signalled a north wind. I was glad I was well wrapped up. Being up and about is a gift, especially when the morning is golden autumnal and you've just recovered from the flu. The way the sunshine slants up your street, into your eyes, it forces you to look down and away from early-morning passers-by. The crackle and crunch of trodden leaves sets up a rhythm. Without knowing why, contemplation takes over. Glory of glories, I was looking forward to going back to work. It must have had something to do with the anti-biotic.

  I crossed the street at the turn-off to St Jude's Nursing

Home for the Elderly. A cloud scurried in front of the sun, as clouds sometimes do. This one put its brakes on and blotted out the sunlight for the five remaining minutes of my walk. The streetscape took on a sharper, more wintry edge. I shivered and looked up. The tips of trees were bare, threatening things, like thorns ready to fall. Behind and above them, the top floor of Jude's beckoned to me from a distance. My mood was darker now, because of the cloud or the proximity of my workplace I could not tell.

Here I was, not even back to work and already wishing my life away, waiting for the next day off. I sighed and tightened my scarf around my head. Life in twenty-first century Dublin was easy for those who were in with the right crowd. You could be in with them too, if you were prepared to compromise. There are those who say you should never compromise, an admirable assumption, but I have found that most people who say that usually have little to compromise about. And so I justified my daily dose of hypocrisy.

I entered the gates of Jude's, heavy in heart, down in spirit. Then I saw Sister. I gave her my doctor's paper, which she examined closely as though it might be forged. "The flu again." She mouthed the last word without a trace of emphasis. "Why don't you get the annual vaccine?" she added. "Now's the time of year for it."

"I do. I get it every June."

My sense of humour was lost on her. She looked at me with the kind of glance a policeman might reserve for a drunk who claims he's got asthma and can't blow into the bag.

"It's great to be back," I said to Jenny as I rinsed my mug in the canteen sink. She gave me that knowing look and mentioned the Clandestine's attack in Drumcondra the previous night. "There was a lot of damage done," she said. "That's the second attack in as many weeks."

I reached for the tea-towel and began to dry my mug. The view was panoramic from the little window above the draining board. Out there somewhere the Clandestines had struck. Church property had been attacked again, no doubt. The Clandestines chose their targets carefully. I mumbled something non-committal about the Clandestine campaign. For months now they had been chipping away at everything ecclesiastical, without seeming to make much impact. Their lack of success was, to say the least, disheartening. The thought of it left me in no mood to make small-talk.

When break was over Jenny said she wanted to introduce me to the new occupant of room 32. "You'll like her. She's lively and alert. Mind you," Jenny glanced at her watch, "she won't be in her room now though. It's nearly lunchtime." With that Jenny opened the canteen door and led the way to the common room.

Twelve-thirty, the busy hour. The mobile ones head for the common room to while away the day-long minutes before lunch. They walk, with or without walking frames, or they glide silently along the corridors in silver-rimmed chairs. Jenny held the door open so I stepped in first. Two categories of old folk sat before me: the helpless and the hopeless. I had learned long ago to avoid eye-contact with the hopeless cases; the seniles and Alzeimers. As for the helpless, they're always slouched in their seats, heads leaning against the backrests, too tired or too doped to look even vaguely alert. Unless of course they're expecting visitors. Then they usually perk themselves up, if only to make their families feel less guilty for not taking care of them at home.

The new recruit to life in a nursing home sat on the far side of the room. Because of where she sat - back to us, staring out the bay windows - and the way she sat - head erect, not touching the backrest - I noticed the back of her head first. It was covered in tiny white curls. The light that day made it look like a thousand silver rings of equal size, equal sheen, were embroidered in her hair. I was admiring the neatness of her hairstyle when she heard our footsteps and glanced around.

"Laura," said Jenny, "this is Nurse Collins."

With one hand Laura lowered her glasses to the bridge of her nose. She looked up at me, the colour of her eyes matching exactly the blue rims of her bi-focals. Her other hand took mine and shook it briefly. Early eighties, I guessed. Her eyes were young and her grip firm.

"Nurse Collins is from Coolock, too," said Jenny.

"Oh. Wherabouts exactly?"

And so we chatted. In the ten minutes before lunch all I found out about Laura was that she had lived in Dublin for most of her days. I couldn't find out anything else. She plied me with so many questions about my own life that I couldn't get a question in edgeways. When the bell went for first sitting she was up, sprightly as a lamb in springtime, heading for the dining room.

Meeting Laura coincided with an uplifting of my spirits that lasted the whole shift-long day. I put it down to her because working with the hopeless and the helpless can be so emotionally flattening - especially when portraits of our great Archbishop stare down at you in every corridor, his creepy eyes following your every move. A resident who is bright, alert and inquisitive is a bonus to be treasured. I wondered how long Laura would last, and hoped it would be for a very long time. I spent the rest of my day in Medication, sorting out pills on trays. Jenny came in to do some stocktaking. As we talked, I developed a cough.

"Are you sure you're over that dose?" Jenny asked.

"Am I ever?" I answered between splutters.

I walked the streets to the bus-stop. Evening's glow draped itself about my back and slowly emaciated my long shadow. Two of the Avenue shops had already shuttered up as I passed. Three of the other outlets were permanently closed these days. The remaining shop, Griffith's, stayed open only because a two-man security outfit constantly patrolled the pavement outside it after dark. I noticed a pair of youths scurrying off through the gloom with two cardboard boxes, doubtless their homes under the shelter of a railway bridge or in the lee of some piss-ridden alley. I hoped for their sakes the security men would not arrive and let the alsatians loose on them. The thought was enough to dampen my mood again as I walked into the darkness of the coming night.

Home. A house just south of the river. The kind of place where neighbours whisper about you across the clotheslines; the inflexibility, the uniformity, the hopelessness of a collapsed economy etched on everyone's face. The kind of estate that might once have been prosperous, in the long-lost days before Ireland lifted up its clerical skirts and retreated into its sad, dark history.

Four of us lived there. I was the only northsider. Maybe every city in the world is split in two: the have's and have-not's, the arrogant and the humble, the suburb and the ghetto. Perhaps, just as every bully needs a victim, so every community needs a butt-end to kick. Dublin is no exception. It has its northside and its southside. After a while you get used to the jokes about northsiders keeping cars on blocks in their front gardens, and the BMW street-races in stolen cars late at night. I had developed a neat line in describing what it was like growing up with herds of wild gypsy horses roaming beneath my bedroom window. 'Beats Montana anytime,' was one of my favourite closing gambits. My way of deflating southsiders was usually successful, but not always. Take Suzy, for instance. I reckoned I got on well with the other girls in the flat, Katie and Niamh, but Suzy grated my nerves. She was so chirpy it was unbelievable. I made allowances - she was ten years younger and still idealistic. She constantly berated me about why I was still a general nurse after fifteen years service, and why I didn't go to Mass every week, seeing as I was working for the Archbishop. She was at it again tonight, so I said, "You'd be able to figure out the answers to your own questions if only you could put two and two together."

"Oh really? You shouldn't have to compromise yourself like that, Pauline."

I'd been waiting for that. I gave her my pet theory about compromising. That really got her going. Have you ever noticed the way southsiders lose their refined accents once the argument gets heated? I listened to her ranting on about hypocrisy. I said that if she was so concerned about compromising she should join the Clandestines. Suzy did not react the way I expected; she stared at me in stunned silence, a penetrating look in her eyes. Katie slammed her mug down on the coffee-table and barked, "Will you two give over?" Niamh threw a glance skyward and upped the television volume with her zapper.

I lay in bed feeling morose. I put my mood swings that day down to my time of the month, but it wasn't that. I thought of Suzy and how right she was. God, how I envied her those good looks and that gravity-defying figure - but then it's hard for someone with tits as upturned as the Queen of Sheba's not to be arrogant. No use in explaining to her that when I was a younger nurse, my liberal views were the real reason for my lack of promotion. "So," she had retorted, "you were one of thousands who pretended to be liberal simply because it was fashionable to do so in those days."

I thought my coffee cup would implode, I was squeezing it so tightly. That was rich, coming from someone who was barely out of nappies back then. When the country lurched to the right after the EU imploded in on itself, there were a lot of black marks put on the files of those with liberal attitudes. Now, in the descending night of pious clericalism, those with clout donned their blackest garb and discriminated against anyone who was less than devout. Jesus Christ, now my mind was racing back over all the day's events. I lay awake, tossing and turning. At some fitful early-morning hour, to the tune of a siren wailing in the distance, sleep came and I grasped it gratefully.

Days shortened. Darkness mercifully cloaked the decaying city as I went to ply my trade beneath the Archbishop's all-seeing eye. I worked late-shift mainly, and found myself coughing and spluttering with increasing frequency, which Jenny put down to the time of year. Two things kept me sane in my job: her and the new resident, Laura. I found out that Laura had gone to Saudi Arabia in the years following her retirement from the civil service. Her only child had taken a nursing job in Riyadh, so in the year following her husband's death, Laura had gone to live with her daughter. We spent many an hour talking about Saudi - especially the men. Laura would sometimes look at me with a devilish gleam in her eye and say, "You don't know the half of it, my dear."

I never quite got to the bottom of what she meant by that. If I asked she would tap knowingly on the side of her nose with her finger and point to the picture of the Archbishop, as if he might somehow be listening. In the early days she often asked me about myself. I told her certain things about my upbringing. As it turned out, we were both from opposite ends of Coolock. Laura had not known anyone in the neighbourhood by the name of Collins. When she realised that the only surviving members of my family were two sisters who had emigrated to Australia and New Zealand, and some aunts with whom I had long since lost contact, she respected my privacy and asked no more. I did tell her that I had spent two years working and travelling in the USA. That was back in the nineties, before I went nursing. We spoke frequently of what had motivated us to each spend some time abroad. "There was a need in us both to get away," she said once, adding that in my case it might still be there. Sometimes she mentioned the future, and where I might be in time to come. She had enough savvy to know I was not happy in my work, and I had enough trust in her not to hide it any more. One day, right under the Archbishop's nose, she asked me what I would really like to do. For the first time in my life I outlined my fantasy to another human being.

I told her I wanted to live in Wyoming, to raise plants there in a small farm on the edge of the prairie. I painted her a picture of me perched in a rocking chair on a verandah beneath the great blue sky, my pet raccoons at my feet, watching the live-long day go by.

She laughed and said, "That's all very well, but what about a man?"

"Who needs one?" My mood changed as a face came into my mind. Martin of the golden hair and silver tongue. Sly Martin, Martin the Bastard, Martin who had me drawing up an invitation list only to discover, at the last possible moment, that he was already married... I snapped out of it: "I've had enough men to do me for a while," I added. Laura never mentioned them again.

Three things attracted me to Laura - the hint in her of a wild and carefree youth, which age had not entirely extinguished - her independence of spirit in the soul-sapping environment in which we talked - and the realisation that she had no visitors, her daughter having died some years before. Sometimes I saw pools of loneliness in her eyes, pools so deep they touched me to the bone. When I asked if there was anything she particularly wanted for Christmas, she requested a pair of budgies in a cage. Ein and Stein she called them. What joy their chirpings brought. We fixed them up with cuttlebones and mirrors. Laura watched them perch and preen, and preen and perch. She sang to them until they too began to sing. In their company, the loneliness and emptiness of a nursing home existence became more tolerable. Time passed more consolingly for Laura now in these, the winding-down days of her life. Then one cold January day, Sister sent for me and said that the birds were an annoyance, the residents couldn't enjoy their afternoon naps, and to please inform Laura that they were to be got rid of forthwith.

I still see Laura's kitten-soft eyes. The cleaning lady who took the birds away promised they would get a good home. I volunteered to take them myself, but Katie and Niamh objected - the landlord would have a fit. Birds were noisy, dirty things. Who would clean out the cage? I replied that there was so much shit around here already that another little bit would make no difference. That killed my chances stone dead.

I clung to a strap on the 191 bus. The bridge was clogged with traffic; the night was cold, and the windows fogged with the streams of rush-hour condensation that only a wild, wet, wintry night in Dublin can produce. I hung there, wondering what crime this busload of humanity had committed to deserve this. An old man at a window seat had a cough so deep it rattled around his ribcage like a motorbike on a wall of death. Someone wiped a window and the slosh of water was clearly audible. All around me passengers clung like rag-dolls to the straps of the overcrowded bus. Scrawny schoolkids bawled obscenities so loud that my eardrums ached and I knew I was coming down with something. The bus jolted forward. Hot breath rolled down my neck like warm jam. Something hard rubbed against my hip. I looked around and there was a middle-aged man pretending not to look at me, a leery grin pinned to his face. The bus jolted again and the tip of my umbrella in a sore place solved the problem alongside me. I got out at the next stop and walked the rest of the way home, letting the rain soak me. I arrived home to the news that Suzy had moved to a flat somewhere in the deeper south-side. Katie and Niamh told me that first, then gave me their 'we've been thinking' look. I said nothing, showered, and went to bed.

Laura began to slip soon after Ein and Stein were taken away. Sometimes they go very quickly. I could see it in her walk. She was stooped now, requiring the assistance of a cane. In her eyes I saw the onset of that dreaded look, the laminated look that comes over all the residents sooner or later. She was one of them now, the hopelessly bewildered. I watched her become a swimmer in the darkness, her mind a metronome swinging to its own sad tune, its own unknowable time. She would start to talk gibberish about the desert, thinking she was back in Saudi with her daughter. In moments of quasi-lucidity, she would grasp my hand in her bony fingers and say, "It's my money they're after. They want me to will everything to the Church."

"I know," I said. "That's what they do with everyone." It was the truth, I knew. I was rapidly approaching the point where I didn't care who heard me saying it.

The flu-bug took me in its arms again. God, how I wished I could find some way of ridding myself of that damn virus. It didn't seem to affect other people half as much. "The propensity for colds and flu is not shared equally among everyone. Some are affected more than others. Once you shake this off, who knows, you mightn't get another dose for years." That's what the doctor said. I felt like telling him where to shove his propensity, especially with the dose that was on me. Two weeks it lasted this time.

I failed to notice that Spring had come to the tree-lined avenue as I walked the turn-off to Jude's on my first day back. I saw no buds. I only had eyes for the sharp, pointy things that hung over me like sabres. When I saw the top floor of Jude's beckoning in the distance, I felt sick once more.

Before I had time to change into my uniform, Sister ordered me to her office. She said my rate of absenteeism was not acceptable. I countered that all my illnesses were certified by doctors, that anyone was entitled to be sick. She said it was more than that. It was my attitude. "How can you work in a Catholic nursing home?" she said.

I looked at the gravelly lines on her face, at the picture of the Archbishop on the wall, at the Child of Prague standing in its chipped glory on a shelf, and thought how can I indeed?

I told Jenny over coffee in the canteen.

"You mean you're sacked?" she whispered, incredulously.

"That's right, my contract won't be renewed. I've a month left."

"Jesus, Pauline. What'll you do?"

"I've no idea. She told me I could stay on as a cleaner."

"The bitch..."

"Sssssh, I think this place is under surveillance, you know - listening devices? Keep your voice down, Jenny. If they think you have an attitude problem, they'll find some excuse for sacking you too. You can't afford to lose your job, not with a husband and two small sons to look after."

"I don't care. She's still a bitch."

"I find it hard to work up any sort of contempt for Sister," I said. "I mean, she's just a cypher in the system. I'd feel more contempt if I had any respect for her. But I don't. Never had, actually. She knows how I feel. She can't take it."

"Did you tell her how you feel?"

"No, that would be treating her with something like respect. She'd love me to lose my head and start ranting and raving in front of her, but I won't - and that kills her."

"What will you do?"

"I've no idea. Oh, I didn't tell you my other good news. I have to find a place to stay as well."

"What? Why?"

"The two harpies from the southside - you know, Katie and Niamh - seems they and I didn't get along as well as I thought. They told me at the weekend that they want to bring in two pals now that Suzy's gone awol. Trouble is, the landlord won't allow more than four stay in the house."

"When have you to leave?"

"The end of the month."

"Pauline," Jenny reached across the table, took my hand in hers and said, "I don't know what to say...I..."

Jenny was magnificent, a friend to die for. She kept me sane that month by telling me over quiet drinks in dark pubs that my troubles were blessings. She told me her theory that the job was driving me mad anyway. The people I was working for were firewalking on the embers of my soul, twisting me, destroying me. My illnesses were a symptom, she said. So was my cynicism. It had been eating me up, stressing me out, burning me out. I didn't have the mechanisms to cope with it, like she had. Now that I was on my way out of it, I'd feel better. It was the same with the house. I had never been remotely happy there. My enforced change was for the better, she said. It had been my inbuilt inertia factor that had kept me from leaving all the time, she said.

She was right, though two things happened - one to scare me, one to sadden me - before the month was up. The fright came when I answered a loud knock on one of my last nights in that southside household. Two policemen stood at the door. My immediate thought was that Sister had sent them to take me away, but they were there to quiz me as to Suzy's whereabouts. She had left no forwarding address, I said, which was the truth. They went away and I lay in bed that night, wondering why they might have been looking for her, and wondering what she might be getting up to these days, with her hourglass figure and alpine tits.

That night I resolved to track Suzy down. I knew it would not be easy to find her. My only clue was something she had said once about spending Saturday afternoons at Newtown Gate Market.

Three hours I waited. There was this guy at the market entrance, a flute-player. His lilting tunes helped pass the time. Just when I'd given up hope, Suzy appeared from the far side of the street. She looked at me, startled.

"Can I treat you to a coffee?" I said. "There's something I want to talk about."

She looked around once, twice, three times. "Why?" she hissed.

"I've lost my job."

The look of suspicion cleared from her eyes, at least momentarily. "Why?" she said again.

"Let's go in here," I pointed to the cafe.

"Conor comes too," she nodded to the flute-player.

I bought three coffees and got straight to the point by telling Suzy that a god-squad had come looking for her the previous week. My colloquial description of the moral policemen didn't faze her one bit. "Did they say why they were looking for me?" she asked.

"No, they didn't." I shrugged a little and muttered something about reports in the paper that the police were rounding up Clandestine sympathizers.

Suzy glanced at the flute-player. He sipped his coffee. Something told me that he was the strong, silent type. We spoke about my job then, how I had been given one month's notice. That seemed to open things up a lot as far as Suzy was concerned. She became downright friendly. After another round of coffee, she gave me a phone number and told me there might be some work available.

The sadness that was becoming increasingly inevitable came two days before the end of my final month. I held Laura's hand in mine. I held it tightly in those final moments before the pale blueness of her eyes closed forever. She was gabbing on again about Saudi Arabia. In the last minutes her mind cleared, as if girding itself for the great leap that awaited it. She grasped my fingers to the bone and rasped, "I left them it all... All twenty euros...."

I cried and laughed and coughed and spluttered all at the same time. The stroke had paralyzed her left side. Her right hand clenched mine again. Out of the corner of her mouth she hissed, "There's a letter in the drawer for you... There's something for you... It's..." She surrendered to the night then, the all-enveloping night. Somewhere in that deep blue sky where budgies fly, a new note sounded and a new song was sung.

Before the porters came to wheel her out of room 32, I went to Laura's drawer and found the letter. My name was scrawled across it in the spindliest handwriting I had ever seen. I felt what was in it and knew it was money. I took it out and examined it. It did not amount to much, but to me it was worth more than all the riches in the world. I looked at the Archbishop's portrait, and something made me think of living in Wyoming. Fuck Wyoming. How stupid a fantasy, how ridiculous that after all these years I was still working beneath a cold-eyed cleric in a god-forsaken nursing home. Fuck escap*ism*, it was time for escap*ing*. I thought of Jenny and her inner strength, how she could cope and I could not. I thought of Suzy, how she had taken on a new life in the shape of the Clandestine cause. Those coffees in the marketplace and a few discreet questions had brought me to the threshold of an organisation that was intent on destroying everything that I had devoted the best years of my working life to. I thought of all that, and in one crazy moment my eyes swivelled from the Archbishop on the wall to the letter in my hand to the corpse on the bed. Somewhere in that sequence, somewhere between arrogant prelate and cold death, my head spun and something gave.

Something small as a feather on a budgie's tail. Something to steer by, to live by. Something small as a speck of silica in the shifting sands of desert time, in the desert far away. The desert was here now, right here in room 32. Laura was here too, her soul swooping low over the Saudi sand, revisiting it one last time. In the closing moments of her death-flight to something new, something better, her tail feathers stirred the sand and brewed it up into a storm. Tiny grains stung my eyes. Each speck imprinted its own image in my brain.

I saw Sister's gravelly-lined face. Her Child of Prague sat on her right shoulder like a demon-angel to beseech me; the Archbishop peered out from behind her left shoulder to threaten me. I saw Suzy and her friend, Conor, fighting for what is good and right; I saw the 191 stuck in a jam on the bridge; I saw Jenny's boys growing big and strong. I saw it all, what is right and what is wrong, what is good and what is bad. Somewhere between the incubus and succubus of all my days, between the formative and the cumulative, I knew that the time had finally come for me to make a choice. In the making and the choosing, life's baggage fell from my shoulders. The flu-bug and the cynicism fell too. As I snapped out of whatever it was that had taken hold of me, I thought it ironic that I should feel so good, so healthy, in a room, a home, so full of death.

I took off my uniform for the last time that shift. I walked out of the nursing home, never to return. Two days later, after putting flowers on Laura's grave, I rang in sick. "The flu," I said to Sister. Then I put the phone down and walked away.

UPLANDS

Beneath the fiery moons of Arkon lay the city of Alchazar. Above its dome-shaped roofs and balconies flowed a Dreambeam, encircling the planet like a lifebelt on a star. In the Uplands on the far side, a three-eyed Lymphet stood and stared. Bewildered by confusion, in a welter of despair, he sought to know, "What has happened to the Dreambeam? Why can't I see it any more?"

Without waiting for an answer he turned to his companion, a creature of great renown. "Wise One, can you tell me what brings this blight upon my eyes? My heart is stricken by the emptiness that fills the distant skies."

"The skies are not vacant," the Elder Lymphet pointed with outstretched hand. "Behold the stars and stellar clouds, the planets and the moons..."

"Wise One, let me clarify what I mean. I speak not of suns and galaxies, but of what has become of the Dreambeam."

The Elder sat upon a rock considering his reply.

"Leave to one side matters you cannot see and contemplate instead that which can be seen. When you have reflected on things tangible, ask yourself, 'Is that which is real, solid and visible more important than that which is indefinable, uncertain and unseen?' If your answer is yes, then return to Alchazar contented. If your answer is no, then return to the city in the knowledge that you will never find happiness."

The younger Lymphet obediently turned from the wise one and cast his gaze across the Arkon nightscape. Silently he let his mind reflect on all that lay before him. From his isolated eyrie in the Uplands, a compelling vista awaited his inspection. To the north a snow-peaked range of Polar Hills sparkled beneath the stars, its rugged clefts and cols illuminated by fountains of lava that flared and faded as magma erupted from deep volcanic wells.

The Polar Hills rose like a derelict becalmed in a vast sea of lava, its surface hidden in darkness. Somewhere in the dim distance, the lava fields became the beautiful Plains of Javlon, which shimmered westward, iridescent and smooth, to Alchazar. To the south lay fertile valleys, their rich and lazy contours a soothing panacea to the pyrotechnics of the north.

The deep red light of Arkon's largest moon was almost all-pervading. It permeated the cleavage in the Uplands where the younger Lymphet turned his triple eyes to a firmament full of planets, moons, starry fields and galactic clouds, but devoid of Dreambeams.

Presently, the Lymphet lowered his head. No longer contemplating the skies, he stared instead at the rocky soil beneath his feet. He stood forlorn, swaying despondently.

The Elder sensed a need to extol. "Why worry about ephemera? You hold a position of respect in Alchazar. You do not want for things material. Think of your offspring - will there not be joy in rearing them? Are you not contented with your niche and your good fortune?"

"Oh Wise One, it is not a question of being satisfied with my lot. It is less an affair of what I am, more a matter of what I'm not."

His corrective tone rankled the Elder. "Bad enough that you speak in rhyme. Must you also speak in riddles?"

"It's so hard to explain. I'm successful, my life is secure, but the nub of the problem is: I wish there were more. These dreams that I look for, you call them ephemeral, I know for a fact they are real and attainable."

"Nonsense!" The Elder turned to his left, addressing a boulder as if seeking to admonish elusive spirits skulking within. "The Dreambeam exists only to feed our imagination when we are young. As we ripen it grows dim. When we reach maturity it fades into nothingness. We are ready for the world when we realise that the Dreambeam ceases to exist. Do not dwell on it for it will bring you trouble. It is merely the stuff of myth. Meditate instead on your position in society. Reality consists of what you see around you."

"You tell me, Old One, to reflect on the responsibilities of my position. But what if such concerns do not satisfy my ambition?"

The Elder stood, grim-faced and stern, the hair-like growth covering his body bristling with anger. "Come!" he said. "Enough of this."

But the younger Lymphet stayed and turned once more to face the moonscape. Between the twin satellites of Arkon, he glimpsed a curving effervescence indicative of one thing. Filled with overwhelming desire, his third eye opened.

The Dreambeam revealed itself in a multiplex of splendid visions. A celestial hall of mirrors, an abracadabra of orbital optics, paraded before his eyes. Faraway places tumbled across aurora-filled skies in a dazzling arc-like display. On a floating ocean, cargoes of gold sailed through cloudbursts of silver. Kaleidoscope coastlines speckled with clusters of walking plants blended into valleys suspended in rainbows. Above these a great tumulus through which a tunnel led to a dark side where unspeakable dangers lurked. Beyond, hidden behind the water veils of Ephrael, the Lymphet knew he would find destiny.

Turning to his teacher, he said, "I ask one favour. Will you look me in the eye and deny that the Dreambeam exists? Will you tell me it's a lie?"

The once venerable one shuffled past, not daring to meet the younger Lymphet's gaze.

"You refuse to affirm or deny. Why?"

Hair-like skin hanging limp and listless, the Elder halted two paces from the cliff-edge. His baleful reply floated westward over the Plains of Javlon. "Very well," he said. "I will tell you. The Dreambeam is real and visible but only to those with faculties to see it. As we grow older, our third eye, the one above the other two, grows dim until finally it sees no more. This is the eye that sees the Dreambeam. That is how the Dreambeam fades from our consciousness. We are not aware of when our third eye ceases to function. On the contrary, because it remains physically intact and unaltered we assume it still sees. In reality it becomes a mere facade; worthless, defunct, like an artificial jewel or a mummified bird. There are some who succeed in re-opening that eye. I suspect you are one. If that is so I have nothing left to teach you, for now you are better and wiser than I." With a poignant emptiness in his voice, the Elder added, "Go then. Leave this old and useless mentor to his mortification, for I was once like you, but to my shame I shirked my destiny."

Arkon nightscape changed subtly. A rising sun diluted the blood-red rays of moonlight. The jagged Uplands came more into focus. Blurred edges sharpened as dawn's pale incandescence chased shadows from crevices. Crags were illuminated, cracks were illuminated - including the cracks in the cliff-edge beneath a disconsolate and now pathetic Elder. The rockface below the once wise one fell sheer for fifty metres. Becoming less steep, it flattened into surrounding plains.

*   *   *

At the point where the Uplands joined the plains there was a bed of scree; the product of aeons of pebbles discarded from the rocks above. Looking proud and dignified, the Lymphet stepped among the rubble. Bodycoat erect and glistening in the morning glow, he paused to contemplate the far horizon. Rising from the lava fields beyond the plains were the Polar Hills. In that farthest of faraway places he knew there was a stairway to a Dreambeam, a gateway to a new world.

OBLIVION FADE

The man with the trembling hands shelters from the rain in the lee of an old ash tree. Man and tree stand crumpled and bent; one from the howling of prevailing winds, the other from the hounding of advancing years. They lean in the same direction, man and tree, but ash is pathetic, seepy and weepy, it provides nothing like the sustained shelter of broad-canopied oak.

There are no oaks on this rocky slope, only skinny trees with sieves for leaves. Through web-like rain the man sees the Hill of Howth cloaked in distant mist. Fluid and tactile, rain slithers through the leaves. Its spidery filaments twitch ever so slightly as they engulf the bay with the same mist that enshrouds Howth. Now the rain threatens Bray Head, that great lump of rock jutting out of the sea like a giant's tumulus a few miles off the man's right-hand shoulder.

The bay captures his gaze, its broad sweep hiding and nurturing the river that glides somewhere through the grey city below the hills. The city, too, is moistly veiled. This is old rain, rain of centuries, rain of a lifetime. In its drops he sees the city, and a life that was.

He was once an oak, strong and solid as old Dutch furniture, much sought after, not to be pushed around lightly. Certainly not to be pushed around in the media centre where he worked. In those offices down by the river, Simon Thornton was in an element where dreams are made. He had been in on digital TV from the start and had worked his way up. More than his career gratified him - in the days and nights beyond his fifth floor workplace, Dublin gifted him a glow as keen as the delight on a child's face after a roller coaster ride. The city was like that in those far-off days. A zillion sybaritic cranes on its skyline heralded the birth of a new affluence. Beneath the stalking cranes the city became the new Barcelona, the new London, the new Paris. Capital of music, of fashion, of entertainment, of everything that dared to be cool in the heat and light of the new media. Over two decades, Simon Thornton moved from twenty-something cutting-edge to middle-aged lynch-pin of the entertainment industry.

A piece of Simon remained aloof from the corporate self-image of those in the new media. This indefinable part of his personality - a hazy kink way out on the edge, undetectable unless you knew him well - was destined to remain blurred even to him. He knew it merely as a legacy of his father and of his grandfather before him. It manifested itself in his pursuit of old first editions - not just books of any sort, but those of a particular type: crime novels. Simon's favourite possessions were rare copies of Chandler and Elroy from the twentieth century. His passion for reading and collecting did not rest easily with the interests of his peers. They marked him out as being an oddball. They knew he spent his spare time foraging through the second-

hand bookshops and auction rooms of Dublin - a public manifestation of the kink that kept him from becoming a company
lapdog; that made him disdainful of corporate achievement
awards; that distanced him from spending weekends in execu-
tive pursuits such as ripping around on noisy wave-riders, tearing up the bay and the mountain lakes.

The mountain lakes lay behind him now, in every sense, and
were filling up fast with rain. The old man wondered how long
he could stay beneath this god-forsaken clump of ash before
pneumonia set in. No longer an oak, these days a husk, the con-
genital march of arthritis in his limbs, the coronary symbiosis of
quickening years and shortening breath reminded him of what
might come he knew not when, except that it might come soon.

Hawk's wings hovered in grey-lit sky. He heard them flut-
tering overhead like an undertaker shaking the veils over a
rigouring corpse. How strange it is: a life spent climbing the
achievement ladder, and how will it all end? With him saying
something obscene about Irish weather before keeling over in a
welter of snot and phlegm?

'That wetting up the mountains got him in the end', they will
say.

What matter? There are no good ways to go, only sad ways.
No difference between a slow burn in a cancer ward and being
squashed to death by a juggernaut. All pain is relative. To some,
the dull ache of a meaningless life is as painful as the searing
march of cancer cells. It is those we leave behind who decide the
quality of our exit.

Karen Mooney stood up. With a downward sweep of her hands
she straightened her short skirt. "Mr Sutherwood will see you
now, gentlemen," she said, a crimson flourish of her long fingernails indicating the boardroom off the lobby behind her desk.

Simon Thornton winked at her as he and his three colleagues walked into the inner chamber. She offered him the coquettish smile she had been trained not to flash at her superiors. Simon did not mind. He could tell that she was wearing *Masque*, lashings of it. She closed the door behind them, consigning four company executives to a meeting with the man who was their future, the future of mass entertainment.

Sutherwood offered no words of greeting, only a back-throated *sit down* as he rested his chin on his hands. Like a year-head at a meeting of prefects, he stared momentarily at each of them, at their power-sitting postures. He swivelled in his chair to the wall-screen behind him and began to outline the next quantum leap in broadcasting technology. It was the obvious step after digital, after the internet, after the mobile phone. No one would mislay anything any more, or forget to switch it on. It would be harmless, he promised.

"Large scale communication will be possible," he declared, the wall-screen lighting up with visuals. "Thousands of channels will be available - radio and TV, as well as libraries of stored music and films. Mobile contact will be instantaneous - phones, cellular and landlines, will become redundant. Networking can be jacked in too, rendering screens and monitors largely unnecessary. Think of the office space companies will save!"

Simon saw the future that day. He saw it sculpted in the lines on Sutherwood's face like omens etched in stark calligraphy - no room for questions, no shadows where suspicion might skulk. He found himself asking about side-effects and the quality of the material that would be made available on the channels. His three colleagues shifted in their seats; edging ever so slightly away from him, isolating him in front of the most powerful man in the world.

Sutherwood smiled his charming smile. Warm-hearted as a freshwater pike, he re-adjusted his spectacles with his left hand. Simon had seen the mannerism several times before. He knew those old-fashioned round-rimmed designer glasses made a fair attempt at masking the crows' feet around Sutherwood's eyes. They failed to hide the callousness lurking within. They magnified it. With a throwaway rub of his hands Sutherwood glared and said that what the people wanted is what they would get, despite do-gooders and wooly-minded intellectuals.

Not for the first time Simon wondered why he had let his mouth run away with his tact by querying the Sutherwood ethos in front of the man himself. He knew his concerns might slow down his career curve. It had always been a flaw with him, this inability to keep his mouth shut. He knew his three colleagues wished their leather-backed swivel seats might swallow them to spare their embarrassment. Simon knew they would never lose the tacit finesse of grovelling before the great man, the founder of the empire that seemed to be spreading everywhere. Sutherwood had the status of kings. Those around him were kingmakers.

Simon Thornton opted to curtail his treason and remain part of the regime. He shrunk into his own chair while those about him took control of the meeting. Sutherwood was not evil, Simon knew that. He was just a hard-nosed businessman taking over the planet. As Sutherwood droned on about time-scales and five-year plans, Simon looked out through the windows of the media corporation's hermetically-sealed offices and wondered if he had opened his big mouth one time too many. In the distance the haughty cranes of Dublin stood motionless in the breeze. Down the windowpane flowed wispy tracks of rain.

The downpour lifted its veils now. The old man looked out over a rocky outcrop to where a sunburst split the distant sky. The twin chimney stacks of the Pigeon House appeared magically above the horizon. The spit of land beneath them lay draped in mist. A great powerhouse floated in the sky, a surreal gift of light and cloud. It cheered his spirits to see a sight so rare. Momentarily, he forgot the dampness clinging to his neck.

*   *   *

In a club off Liffey Street, within a crane length of his fifth-floor office two weeks after his understated disagreement with Sutherwood, Simon Thornton met the woman of all his dreams. When a wizen-faced cynic passes his forty-ninth birthday, as Simon had three days previously, it was not possible, he knew, to fall in love unless it was socially incorrect.

Yvonne was a dental receptionist, ten years younger and the wrong partner for a high-powered media administrator. But her looks were well-preserved, and she was a fan of the latest technology unveiled by Sutherwood. What fused Simon's interest in her was that she too was a hoarder of books, though few of them were of the crime variety. Her northside apartment was home to over four hundred novels, including a few South American and African authors Simon had never expected to see among so many romances and blockbusters. He had never fallen in love before, not even in the lead-up to his first marriage and not in the eight years since the divorce. With his only child gone to Australia, and his career on a siding since his meeting with Sutherwood, Simon was ready for one great bruising of the soul. In a world he increasingly hated, he knew it would be imprudent to become involved with a dental receptionist. No schoolboy crush, this was true love driven with the exhaltation of bittersweet adulthood.

Simon saw Yvonne as hard-nosed and straight-talking, a woman who had known her share of disappointments. He guessed that life had taught her to be wary of middle aged men, especially when they re-filled her wine glass as often as he did. The evening he first took her to his apartment, he hoped she realised it was friendship he was after, not a one-night stand.

As soon as they were inside he poured her a generous glass of *Cabernet*. Taking her jacket, he said, from behind her back, that he had something to show her. Delighted at seeing his words make her tighten her grip on the glass-stem, he waited for her to turn around. She smiled with relief that his trousers were still zipped up. Delighted that she too had a sense of humour, Simon put his wine on the coffee table before showing off his Chandlers and Hammetts and all the other treasures on his book-lined walls.

It took him weeks to mention that his career was on a slow train to nowhere. By then Yvonne had fallen in love too, realising that what he lacked in looks and sex appeal, he made up for with personality and what she saw as status of the loftiest kind. Simon knew their relationship was serious when one day over lunch she offered to log all his books onto computer for him. They deserved to be listed alphabetically, she said, just as she kept an up-to-date catalogue of her own books. Both lists would remain separate files - of course, she added rather quickly. Of course, said Simon. He poured her a Java from the cafetiere as she told him the latest gossip from the dentistry. He was a good listener. She was fiery and full of chat. Together they danced and drank the nights away in a city full of younger faces. Two lonely corks bobbing on a sea of loneliness, the oldest swingers around, they partied and had fun. And then they married.

Simon chose to remain part of the sleazy corruption of mass-TV. No longer regarded as a vital cog, he was promoted sideways out of the mainstream into a blind-alley miles from the latest developments. He worked out the remaining years of his career with blinkers on. Though he knew they barely tolerated him, it was worth it for the money. It was worth it for Yvonne.

One day, not long after she had finished cataloguing all his books onto disk, she said she wanted to be one of the first with the chip. Simon was not keen but he could never refuse her anything. With his connections it was easy to arrange one of the earliest implants. Yvonne was in and out of the clinic in no time. A TV crew interviewed her as she emerged. They asked did it work and what it felt like and was it worth it and did she think it would change her life. She replied in her feisty way that she was thrilled and never felt so great. They showed her on the six o'clock news, all smiles and wide-eyed, after a report from their scientific correspondent on how the procedure had been carried out.

Biosensors had embedded the chip beneath the skin above her ear. Antigens bonded with antibodies, distorting the membranes of the brain, releasing chemicals that caused complex neural functions. The result was a flow of communication between the cerebrum and the implanted chip. Yvonne could now tune into any radio station, consult any encyclopedia, call up any recording in her head. With a mental command she could flick through the TV channels, watching them in her mind. She could turn everything off with just a thought. She urged Simon to get it done because the new technology might soon allow them jack in to each other, that their minds could become one.

Simon shook his head and kept putting off the date of his own implant. He had turned fifty and was nearing retirement. Though still in love, their relationship had lost its earlier *frisson*. They could say no to each other now, their marriage clogging up with the self-sufficiency that is the dread of all true lovers of a certain age. There was enough clutter in the world, he joked, without plugging it into his own brain. She chided him and on the occasion of their first anniversary sent him a card with a poem in it that she had written herself. It was called *Mechanical Aid*.

Here it comes
Yet it means nought to me
How little effort can be made
With one small mechanical aid.

It's hard to tell what makes it tick
Yet with one swift kick
Its very presence can persuade
My troubles to oblivion fade.

*   *   *

Simon Thornton pushed through the gorse to the road, repeating over and over to himself those last two prophetic lines. Mantras of oblivion in his mind, he saw as he walked to his car that the Pigeon House had been lost in the rain that came streaming down once more. It spurted over the car-lock as he inserted his key. His hands trembled again, perhaps from the cold - maybe it was the onset of another disease. He fumbled with the key until the door opened, clumsily removed his jacket and tossed it on the passenger seat. He took the wheel in both hands to steady them and stared at a windscreen alive with sluicing rain. It snaked down the glass. In each globule he saw history - the silvery promises of history, the silky snakes of history. He sat there staring at them, watching them, believing them, re-living them.

He shook himself and glanced in the rear-view mirror. His remaining hair stood like clumps of frost-covered corn in a bedraggled field. He flattened the yellow-grey crop with one hand. For Simon Thornton, the harvest time of his life had long passed. Arms stiff with the arthritic tension of winter, he sighed deeply and ran his fingers along the inside of his collar in a vain attempt to dry his neck. It was no use. He was soaked through. He remembered Sutherwood's promises, those snaky promises that were oh-so-true for many years. And then.... True like the Earth is flat, like H is for wholesale, like the Irish weather is predictable.

The smoky promises of Sutherwood.

Antibody-antigen reactions worked smoothly, resulting in the dendril-neurone alterations so necessary for perfect reception. Soon the world opted for implants, at least that part of the world living in the booming comfort of the West.

Everybody had them in their heads then:

Bungee-jumping-gravity-defying-weather-babes. Pets-at-risk. Pitter-patter-shock-jocks. The-royal-family. Health-scares.

Celebrity-cooks. Manic-quizzes. Make-over-shows. Cops-docs-and-frocks. Children-with-disabilities. Collectible-fluff. Live-from-Milan: the- latest-fashion-unattainable-to-all-but-the-super-rich. You-can-always-dream. The morning-phone-ins: your-chance-to-make-your-voice-heard. Reality-TV. World's-dumbest-neighbours. Tell-us-about-'em! Cutesey-talk-shows: chat-about-this-yell-about-that-whip-'em-up.

Have you a story to tell us?

My-sister-murdered-my-mother-who-was-really-a-man. The-drama-of-the-cat-caught-up-in-a-tree. Two-headed test-tube-baby-reveals-all. Bulimia: do-you-throw-up-your-meals? Tell-us-about-it-on-the-all-new-Counselling-Channel.

The latest news, local and international:

The-grieving-princess-cuts-short-her-holiday-in-the-Seychelles-to-comfort-her-pony-who-has-broken-its-leg. How-would-you-feel-if-your-children-died-in-a-fire? Well-that's-what-happened-to-a-family-in-Finglas-last-night. For-our-latest-report-we-go-over-to... Live-all-day: the-courtroom-case-of-the-woman-accused-of-shoplifting-in-Spain. We-ask-*you*-did-she-really-do-it? Should-Prince-Harry's-illegitimate-son-be-in-line-for-the-throne? Press-the-red-button. Press-the-red-button. Press-the-red-button.

Soaps:

Docu-soaps. Frothy-soaps. Pseudo-soaps. Serious-soaps. Soaps-that-make-you-happy. Soaps-behind-me. Soaps-in-front-of-me. Soaps-to-the-left-of-me. Soaps-to-the-right-of-me. Soaps-of-St-Patrick-bless-and-protect-me. Banish-those-soapy-snakes-from-slithering-down-the-windscreen...

Simon witnessed the changes that came as society lost its cutting edge. Imagination became pariah, unrewarded by the mediocrity of global media. Attention was lavished on all that was useless. The vital, the profound, the sacred - all were demonized, reduced to feeble non-entity.

The subsequent dumbing down of public expectation led to an overdose of mass entertainment. Movie and music industries aimed their products at the lowest common denominator. Specialist bookshops closed down as publishers went mass-market. Other than roms, they published only soap novels - especially ones between pink or lavender covers. Full of dialogue, afraid of descriptive passages, short on extrapolation; these were televisual books - hard copies of the spoken word, the visual image. The booksellers of Dublin, those that were left, no longer stocked rare old first editions. Simon searched their bargain-bins in vain. Thought-provoking material disappeared like yesterday's news. In a world increasingly inept, economies weakened. Authorities responded with stringent laws and violent discipline. Booming comfort became hardline depression. Simon saw these changes and lived through them. To know what caused them, he had only to look at Yvonne.

He walked again at midnight across an icy bridge one winter long ago. Yvonne slipped and fell against him. He held her in his arms, the inviting press of her face chilled and vulnerable, the all-seeing patina of her eyes probing deeply. He kissed her until she was as warm as a squirrel in a palm tree. He recalled other nights in a vibrant city where celebration stood on stalks like cranes entwined with Christmas lights, where Yvonne, resonant with the hopes and dreams of the city around her, danced for him and made love to him. Looking at her now, planted in her living-room dream-chair like so much flotsam in mud, steel pincers squeezed his heart dry.

For hours she would sit, her green eyes full of nothing but the all-nourishing screen inside her head, her fieriness replaced by a dull compliance - no worries, no cares. The screen piped its values into her brain, making her listless and inattentive to anything but it. "Shut up," she would say, "I'm watching." He would look at her, though he could hardly bear to, and see her closed eyelids wide-screened with the triviality that dominated and moulded her mind until it was full of nothing but a vacant rattiness, a dull acceptance of the mind-consuming images in her head.

Simon Thornton voice-prompted the ignition and drove down the hill. It was as if the window-wipers only partially cleared his windscreen. A film of oily filth coated his vision. No matter how hard he tried he could not see with clarity any more. It became a mystery to him what the implant had done, what Sutherwood had done. He could no more figure out if the whole media takeover had been a cunning stratagem, or if it had come about by accident, than he could figure out the Mountains of Mourne in the overcast distance. Mourn, indeed, he thought, and tried to concentrate on his driving.

They passed him by then - busloads of commuters estranged from reality; faces to the window, glassy eyed. He at once both hated their apathy and understood it. Outwardly the Dubs were still the same. They continued to slag each other but the edge had left their humour. A chilling emptiness filled their eyes; their hi-ho grins not far removed from painted screams. When the economy crashed their expression remained unchanged. Hi-ho, hi-ho, it's on the dole we go. Sutherwood, who now controlled the government, gladly increased their dole money knowing he would claw it back as the masses continued to feed the pay-per-view habit. Simon Thornton knew that the commuters had been afflicted with more than apathy. Each to his own world, every bus fragmented by scores of different dreams, dozens of differing realities. By the time he had it all figured out, it was too late for Yvonne.

She had been one of them for fifteen years; the zombie-dead - all dissent erased, original thought wiped out. One day Simon could take it no more. He killed her in the mountains - the woman who had loved him and who had once, in the old days when her mind had been vibrant with love and beauty, catalogued all his books with all their crimes. He buried her deep in a wood where she would never be found, a place that only he would know. It was a task carried out with all the forethought of the most professional criminal any author had ever dared to write about. It made him weep tears of lead to do it. There, in the glade-like graveyard of his hopes, all his dreams were nightmares, all his nightmares reality.

Yvonne was never far from his mind, like a ghost not fully gone away. In the grey light of rain he saw her once again, appropriately clad in black and white to match the gloom. She sat beside him as the road curled down to where the auto-glide would take over and drag Simon Thornton back to a city no longer stalked by cranes, but by doom-laden clouds and perilous visions. A city where there was nothing to hearten the aching soul except a diminishing resolve to fight it, to keep fighting it, the all-consuming trigger of indifference inside his head. Her words came back to haunt him, *its very presence can persuade my troubles to oblivion fade.*

They were up and behind him now, the mountains. She was gone from the front seat. He drove on, pulling the rearview mirror askew so it reflected not him, but his sopping jacket on the passenger seat. He could not bear to look at himself any more. He gripped the steering wheel, knuckles white with determination not to glance behind. He squeezed the wheel tighter and vowed never to return to her grave. No, not ever again in the pitiful few years he had left, despite the inertia creeping all over his mind, he would never go back again, never go back again. Then the mountain road joined the auto-glide, and his grip eased.

IN BLUEBERRY HILL

The ear-splintering smack of cue ball on pack startled Doogie into wakefulness. It was a power break. The white ball still spun and a black-jacket biker grinned in satisfaction. Doogie reckoned a ball must have gone down from the break, but before he could check, his gaze was forced into its usual slow swivel in time to the haunting, honky-tonk piano. Once again he found himself staring across a bar-room. His view was peculiarly two-dimensional; as if he stood in an art gallery and the bar was a painting he was studying closely. The scene was there in front of him yet he was not part of it. He was detached, and as his eyes roved out of his control he heard that familiar tune. Soon the tinkling intro was over and Doogie found himself miming those well-acquainted words. The bar was swaying too - it wasn't just bikers: the usual crowd was here.

Another whip-crack of pool balls drowned out one of those

lazy drumbeats. Doogie was surrounded by smoke and the buzz of conversation. Below him a cold beer stood on a table, pearls of condensation dripping from its frothy head. In front of him that pretty barmaid - the weekend barmaid! Doogie prayed it was Saturday night. If it was, there was a chance he would come in - the man, the stranger, the one who might somehow be aware enough to liberate him from the hellish trap that ensnared him.

Doogie's only hope lay in making contact with someone, anyone. It was a task which, until recently, had proved beyond him. But now he knew a man frequented this god-forsaken place - a lone man who sipped his pint slowly on Saturday nights - a man who, more importantly, cocked his ear when Doogie screamed. He might, just might, be in again tonight. If he was, there was a hope that he would hear Doogie scream again. This time the man might do something about it. On such slim foundations Doogie raised all his hopes.

Above him the moon stood still. A sax smouldered beneath the words. Two bikers embraced in the middle of the floor, their hands grasping their leather-clad buttocks in a crude slow-dance. Like bottles bobbing on a stormy sea they jerked from side to side right in Doogie's eyeline. Doogie knew it would be the wind in the willows (second time around) before his eyes would shift to the part of the bar where his liberator might be - that's if he was here tonight. Doogie prayed hard. Saturday night he would be here - would have to be here, and alone - he was a loner just like Doogie. He would be alone and listening. Please let him be alone and listening. Then again it might all depend on what time it was and Doogie had no way of knowing that. Perhaps it was too early. Maybe the man might not be in until later. The sweat poured off Doogie now and he knew it was not just from being overweight and singing.

The sax no longer smouldered; it burned red hot through love's sweet melody in a joyous, steamy celebration. Doogie thought of the lyrics and what they conveyed and his heart bled.

With those eyes he saw all those vows he made, never to be. His thoughts and hopes made him so lonely it was tantric. He would have cried, had they been his eyes to cry with. He thought of Linda, how much he had loved her, how he had seen her one night out for a drink with her friends. She had not seen him, though she had looked up at a fat man playing piano. In that fleeting, glancing meeting it was almost as if his eyes were real, but the glimpse crushed him with the knowledge that if a devil ever designed a hell, it would be nothing compared to this.

The wind blew in the willows again. Doogie's line of sight moved agonizingly, tantalizingly, along the bar. The high stools were all full, including the one at the end. Was it? Yes! It was him. He was here! Doogie's mind raced. He would have to be quick - not much time after the cymbals and the snap-roll on the snare drum.

Doogie built himself up for the moment that was fast approaching. Every so often, during his irregular two minutes and twenty seconds of consciousness, he would give himself a life by re-living his most precious memories. Sometimes the dark side came through - the death-night, for instance. He never heard the lorry pull up outside the factory doors. The hum of automated pressing machines smothered the sound of the engine. He watched three balaclavas loading up with a truckful of stolen discs. He never saw the fourth raider until it was too late. The hammer crashed down. It cleaved his security man's hat and smashed his skull.

Only two lines left now. Doogie heard the guitar loud and clear. He thought of the previous Saturday night when he had screamed so loud the man on the stool turned around and looked at the jukebox screen - he had definitely heard something. If Doogie could only scream louder, maybe...

Childhood looped and spiralled through Doogie's bleeding head. He saw glimpses of Linda riding down a long, silent escalator.

Doogie stood at the top, waving. Speckled red curtains slowly veiled his eyes. Soon he saw only darkness. A light, round and bright, appeared at the end of a tunnel. He floated slowly to the tunnel's end. In the bright patch he saw his portrait lingering on the factory floor. His head was haloed in red, a crimson epitaph to a life unfulfilled.

His spirit swayed from side to side, eddying like a feather in a thermal. He could see the upper half of his body now. He could hear the imprint machines pressing discs all around him. By the time his entire body was in view he became aware of one particular set of pressing pistons. His spirit was floating dangerously near to them.

There was nothing he could do. His soul hovered too close to the master disc. Pistons engaged, stamping his spirit forever into the strange, spectral world of the laser. It was an eerie, sleeping world where his only dreams were odd, auroral visions. There was no consciousness, no existence, nothing. His only release was the song now ending. As the final word was sung Doogie mustered his entire spirit for one supreme effort. At this point the singer's eyes always looked at the bar. To his delight Doogie could see that the man, the hoped-for liberator, had his head tilted as if straining to hear something. Doogie would have to be quick. He had less than two seconds between the final note and the all-enveloping blackness that would soon claim him.

Drumsticks rolled on cymbals. A rush of snare signalled the end of the song. The man at the bar thought he heard a distant, high-pitched squeal - something like a scream. Where it came from he could not tell though it seemed to come from behind the wall beyond the video jukebox. It sounded like a scream but perhaps it was a cat. Yes, it was probably a cat. After all, he had heard something like it before - last Saturday night, in fact. As he turned to order another beer, the barmaid smiled at him and the bikers selected something a shade livelier from the playlist.

ZOOM-TIME

It had been building up to a big one all week, so the weather-woman said. She was right. After two days the snow was drift-ing high as hedges. Something in my bones told me it would be around for quite a while.

The hill was impassable by car and damned slippery on foot. No other means of getting to the village below or the manor-house above. Between village and manor stand the stables where I now live, refurbished for human habitation, I hasten to add, by the owner of the manor, the man who rescued me from the gutter, the man for whom I now work. Major Dobbs took me in and gave me food, shelter, employment - not an everyday thing for a man to do, but then Dobbs was always kind. Which makes me wonder how he ever came to be an army officer. I never could figure out how someone as gentle as the major became... a major. The vagaries of the British armed forces have always been a mystery to me. I have found, with people of his class, that their careers are often pre-ordained by family tradition - hereditary, almost. I knew from the start that he would have been a fair-minded, kindly officer (if that is not a contradiction). One look at his eyes and I knew that.

Many months have passed since those eyes first peered at me from the driver's seat of a Range Rover. It was a cold night, though not as bitter as the present snap. The window slid all the way down at an eerie, even pace - electronically controlled no doubt. Just like everything seems to be these days. I prefer manual windows; they usually don't break unless you break your arm. A friend of mine had this car once, the window-electrics stopped working in the middle of a heat-wave. Like driving in an oven, he said - an oven with the door closed. The Rover's electrics were obviously in good working order. The glass disappeared altogether and Major Dobbs said, "How far are you going?"

"Newcastle-upon-Tyne," I lied, "but anywhere down the road will do."

It's a long way from Aviemore to Newcastle, too long for anyone at that hour of a dark winter's night, so I invented my destination in the hope that some kind driver might offer accommodation. I had been on the move around Scotland for weeks then, and had begun to tire of all the travel. I found it easier to get lifts at night. The darkness cloaked my ageing face and tattered clothes. Sometimes drivers pulled away again when they got a proper look at me. I can't blame them for that. Not many want to pick up a tramp. I had become quite good at gauging people's reactions from the look on their face when they realised just what category of person they had stopped their car for. This particular driver didn't bat an eyelid. "Sit in," he said, leaning across to open the Rover's passenger door. At least that bit isn't remote-controlled yet, which is amazing when you consider that boot-doors have been electronically operated in most models for years now. "A cold night for thumbing," he added. The look of more than his eyes, more like his whole demeanour, suggested to me that I had been lucky, very lucky, to have been picked up by him.

Something mellowed in the night-air that wild, highland night. What it was I do not know. Maybe something in the way I answered his many questions made him change his view of the roadside creature sitting alongside him. Perhaps the guilt of generations of landed gentry welled up in him, making him feel that the time had come to reach out across the class divide and do something to bridge the gulf between us. Whatever it was, by Kingussie I knew his name was Dobbs; he knew my name was Joe. By Pitlochry he had offered me a place to spend the night. As we journeyed the last few miles to his manor-home on the shores of the Forth, I knew from his reactions to my answers, my often evasive answers, that he viewed me in the light of one who is fascinated by how a seemingly well-educated and articulate person can end up on Skid Row.

It's a hard place, Skid Row. But the street was never as cold as the Firth of Forth on a freezing January night. Icy sabres rattling in from the North Sea prodded me along the wooded pathway to the stables so kindly allotted to me by Dobbs. I shut the door behind me with a firm dunt of my backside. At least this time I hadn't slipped on the hard-packed snow. I set my bag on the table and pulled my gloves off, undid the top toggles on my duffle-coat, unfurled my scarf, and opened the rest of my coat. I almost forgot to take off my hat. I put it on the back of a chair and felt my beard. It was soft. It froze solid the other evening when I was out walking the major's hounds. After examining my beard in the mirror above the mantlepiece I sat down on the stool. Thankfully the peat-fire still smouldered. I stoked it up with the poker and refuelled it. I thought of all the winos and bums on the other side of the firth. Edinburgh is a cold place at the best of times, unless you have money. I looked around at my one-roomed stables and wondered how much low-life would freeze to death on the streets tonight.

Back all that time ago, on that first, fateful night I met the major, he pulled in at one of those all-night plastic cafes somewhere south of Perth. He said he was hungry, yet barely picked at his meal. He was kind enough to pay for mine though I insisted on paying for the coffees. I could tell that he was having difficulty refraining from asking the question that intrigues most people. Eventually, he asked it: "Back in Ireland, before you ...took to the road, what did you do?"

In the moment of his asking, in the mystical quasi-time between each carefully pronounced syllable, deep down in cavernous plastic, among lumps of coffee undissolved, I saw again a face that haunted me - a face so beautiful my heart ached - as it always did whenever the woman I loved came into my mind. "I was a maths teacher," I said. "Fifteen years I gave it. But I couldn't stand it any longer; the stress got me in the end. There were other reasons too... Do you want more coffee? Refills are free."

He was about to say no but changed his mind. As soon as I brought our cups back I began to tell him what had happened a couple of months previously in Leeds, or rather outside Leeds. I was hitching on a link-road between two motorways. Darkness fell on me. I stood in a lay-by where cars could pull in safely. They did that alright, but not to give me a lift. "It was surreal," I said. "At one point three cars had pulled in all at once, like there was a competition to see who could pick me up first. But as soon as they all slowed down they drove off again in a hurry. I'm used to drivers pulling away once they get a close look, but this took the biscuit. There were so many cars wanting to stop in such a place at such a late hour... Of course I was wondering what was going on. I didn't have to wait long to find out..." Pausing for effect, I slipped a half-empty naggin out of my breast pocket. "Do you take a drink?" I asked.

The major nodded, a slightly nonplussed look on his face as I fortified his cup with a generous drop of scotch. "For the cold," I added, emptying the remaining malt into my own coffee before going on with my story. "A car pulled up on the other side. Two ladies got out and crossed to my side. Two cars stopped; each of the ladies stepped into a different car. This procedure was repeated by another pair of girls a short while later." The major had started to laugh even before I added, "There I was, trying to get picked up at a pick-up point for working girls."

"Well, it was a *lay*-by, wasn't it?"

I had to admire the major's quick-wittedness. He still chortled as he knocked back his coffee. I could see the residue of his previous questioning in his mind. He did not pursue it out of deference to my changing the subject - that was obvious from the look on his face. My whisky-driven antennae were all a-flutter then. When the invisible tendrils of my mind reach out I can tell what's going on in people's heads simply by reading their facial expressions.

"Improves the flavour of roadside coffee no end," the major indicated the contents of my breast pocket. "Better get back on the road. We have another ten miles to go."

Within half an hour he was showing me the door to the stables. "The workmen are still at it so it's a bit rough," he said, "but I'm sure it'll do for the night. Call up to the house in the morning around ten." He was on his way up the path before I could shake his hand. I was about to close the door when he stopped and turned. "By the way, Joe," he called out, "Did you get a lift from that lay-by?"

"No," I said. "I had to walk for miles."

"That's what I thought." His smile sparkled in the moonlight. He turned again and was gone.

That was months ago. In the here and now my peat-fire blazed. To the tune of a whistling kettle I carefully removed a bottle of whisky from my shopping bag. I put it on the counter before switching off the gas. The kettle died with a soft, mournful sigh. I spilled my other messages onto the table. There was butter, ham, cheese and shortbread; these I put away before opening the bottle. I poured myself a long one, adding sugar and hot water until the glass was full. Before taking a sip I carefully examined the other items I had purchased that day. Eight blocks of wood, some small tins of paint and a carving knife that glinted like a razor in sunlight.

Six inches tall, the blocks looked sweet as postcard heather. I held one in my hand and caressed it with my fingers. Somewhere down in the soft-hard workings of my hand, deep in the mysterious ganglia that connect nerve-ends to heart and soul, I felt the essence of a beautiful shape lurking within the wood. A shape would emerge only after long and patient whittling. I longed to start working on the blocks there and then but, too tired to carve, I contented myself to look at the blocks I had already sculpted. Four of them sat on the dresser by the far wall, their features animated by flickering tongues of fire. I sat in the burning peat-light and saw again the face I had seen in the bottom of a plastic coffee cup in an all-night cafe south of Perth. The face that slept in the chambers of my heart was awake now and dancing in the firelight. Her name was Olive - the Golden Olive of my dreams. Olive with her short, blonde hair and hazel eyes. Her specialness to me was all-consuming as naked flame, and just as painful. I saw her then as I had seen her many times, in many guises.

Her face stared down at me from mountainy slopes in Argyll where faraway ridges followed exactly the mounds of her cheekbones, where mysterious caverns and hollows mimicked the treasure troves of her eyes and mouth. In fields of lowland barley her hair tossed and turned with the wind. In fiery sunsets I saw her passion, her nakedness, her love. In deeply mutinous highland lochs, reflections of her face stared up at me. Her mir-

rored image shone out from shop-windows in towns and vil-
lages. I saw them in passing glimpses from speeding cars. I met
her once on the bridge at Inverness, a hundred Olives in the
hands of a balloon-seller. I couldn't believe it, balloons high and
low, each one swaying on a string and on each one the exact
image of my Olive's face. Such glimpses were always illusory;
when I looked again she was gone - except when I stared at the
bottom of a glass or bottle; then she was always there, iridescent, irresistible as whisky distilled from gold.

I sat in the ember-light, warmed by peat and whisky.
Night's silence engulfed me. I thought of other things. The
workmen have finished now; my stables are complete. I have no
radio, no television. The toxic babble of the outer world is
beyond me, for that I am grateful. I hear no more of terrorists
flying planes into buildings; no frenzied child-killers stalk the
streets of my town; no shit-stirring chatshow hosts bombard my
brain with junk - the guerrilla assault of global techno-culture.
No modem traps me in its spider's net. I am an insignificant little fly - a minor irritant, smelly but harmless - hovering over a
horseshit world. Sometimes, in the profound silence of the
night, in the quick-slow zoom-lens of the meditative mind, I see
again that which drove me to the road. That brings to me a sadness no silence can endure. I drink my whisky. When stuporific
sleep comes, I forget.

My ex-wife always said I rambled on too much. I do rabbit on a
bit - excessively so at times, but only sometimes. It was one of
the many reasons she cited for divorce. It wasn't the main one
though. The main reason was younger than me. He was higher
paid, too. My wife's maths went something like this:

Where X= man, Y= woman, and Z= money, find the value of
the following:

$$Y + X + (X + Z).$$

She found the value to be zero.

Her solution was simple:

If $Y + X + (X + Z) = 0$, then $Y + (X + Z) - X = $ Happiness.

Simple - go check the solution on a number line. Verify it with a little piece of paper.

She verified it alright. Another piece of paper took Sheila, James and Robbie. They wanted to stay with their mother. I couldn't argue with that. In my heart I knew they would be happier with her. For a time I hoped for my own solution to divorce, my own path to happiness. Olive was a friend and nothing more, despite the gossiping in the school of rumours where I worked. In time I came to love her, in a sense proving the rumour-mongers right, if only retrospectively. We talked about it one night. I told her I had heard stories of our involvement almost as soon as we had first met. She looked at me across the dinner table. I still hear her soft, plaintive sigh. She grasped the crimson napkin tightly in her hand, smiled ruefully and said, "I never thought of us that way until someone said something once, about us being togeth- er too much."

"Who? When?" I asked.

"About six months after I met you, someone... you wouldn't know who she was. I laughed at her."

"What did she say?"

"That people were talking. That there's no smoke without fire..."

"That's crap. Who was it?"

"It doesn't matter. Like I said, you've never met her. It makes me sad to think that it's not possible for a man and woman to be friends, I mean dear friends, in the society we live in."

Olive raised the cloth napkin to her mouth. She dabbed a dot of chocolate sauce from her lips. The crimson cloth matched precisely the enchanting redness of her lipstick. She placed the napkin back on the table and looked at me in a way that was nothing less than revelatory. Deep in her eyes I saw her wants and needs, I saw them shining from the auricles of her heart. I really thought I could see that far down - beyond the heart even, to the sweet cerebellum of her soul. I saw there a beauty so profound that at that moment I felt a happiness I never thought I would feel again, especially so soon after the divorce.

That was my last visit to a high-class restaurant, except to scavenge for leftovers one bleak night outside a Bradford hotel. That was the nadir of my life on the Row, the night a bar-room bouncer kicked me off the premises. He called me 'scum' to encourage me on my way. No darker cloud has ever enveloped my soul than that which descended on me then. One month in cardboard city, most of it on some developer's tax-dodging bombsite, left me ready for anything, even meths and boot polish. In some strange way that night rummaging in a hotel skip set something off in me. It fired me into a life of constant travel where movement soothed my breast as the road broadened before me. Where the road led I did not care, it was enough that I was on it. The never-ending travel, the constant change of view, kept my mind from atrophying into sorry, sodden molasses. My spirit might have emaciated entirely were it not for the highland vistas that led me to Aviemore. And so I found myself on the A9 one cold night.

When Major Dobbs rolled down his electronic window and offered me a lift, another window also unfurled, one of opportunity to something better. Next morning at ten o'clock I made myself as presentable as possible. As requested, I knocked on the manor door. A young lady, whom I presumed to be a maid, instructed me to go to the scullery entrance. 'Around the side', she said. I was kept waiting for ten minutes before the major appeared. When he spoke briefly, and in a manner more formal than the night before, I not only found myself with a roof over my head, but also a job, of sorts.

Odd Job Joe, that was me. Mending fences, walking dogs, clearing the beats for the salmon season, repairing greenhouses, painting sheds. A mid-day meal was provided, as was the accommodation. The money was pitiful but the welfare topped it up. The citizens of the village viewed me firstly with suspicion, then acceptance of a sort. My fondness for a drop soon became widely known, my daily purchases saw to that. As for buying pots of paint and small blocks of high-quality, imported wood - a dipso, especially an Irish dipso, is liable to spend his shillings on the craziest things...

The only time the major and I spoke at length was at Christmas. Staff-night in the manor-house, no less. Dobbs tackled me for more than an hour, fascinated as much by my capacity for lowering his whisky as for anything I might say. Or so I thought. In a corner of the dining room we spoke. I could still see in him what I had seen in the roadside cafe south of Perth - the curiosity to know exactly why I had given up my former life. "It wasn't just the job?" was how he put it.

"It was a combination of things."

"Like what?"

I shrugged. Behind the major's shoulder, through a baubled blur of pine-needled Christmas tree, the other workers helped themselves to mince pies and a bowl of punch wheeled in on a trolley by the major's niece. It was only recently I found out that she, the one who had opened the door for me my first morning at the manor, was not his maid but his niece. I mentioned this to Dobbs. He laughed and said, "I wish I had the money for a maid. It's not like that these days, Joe. As you can see, all the staff work on the land, except for the cook, of course." Then he said, "You have an incredible capacity to be evasive, Joe."

For some reason my ex-wife flashed into my mind. I blinked and she was gone. "Sorry," I said. "You were saying?"

"It was a combination of things..."

"It wasn't just the work. It was the people I worked with. My marriage failed too."

"Were there children?"

"Three."

"Have you been in contact with them since going on the road?"

"No."

"Was there someone else, Joe?"

I glanced at my malt. The glass was empty. I looked at the major and wondered if the someone he was referring to was my ex's lover, or Olive. Probably my ex's, but one look into the deep pools of his eyes and I caught there one of those pre-ordained insights that the drink plagues me with. Instantly I knew he was speaking of my side of things. He understood. My silence was tacit. "Yes," he said, taking my glass. "I know how you feel. I lost my wife many years ago. Sophie?"

His niece wheeled the punchbowl around the tree and took my glass. She was about the same age as my son Robbie - sixteen, give or take six months. Her long, brown hair fell over her eyes as she poured out a scoopful. She handed me my drink, tossed back her hair, and pushed the trolley away. When she was out of earshot, Dobbs said, "Sophie's mad keen on horse-riding, you know. She's all I have, Joe. All this - the house, the land - means nothing. She's my nearest relative..." In the distance, beyond the yuletide music and Christmas chatter, a shrill telephone rang out. I followed the major's gaze and saw his niece go to answer the call. Knowing it was for him, the major looked at me squarely and said, "You have a job and you have a roof over your head, which is more than what you had, Joe - and less than you deserve." While I was trying to figure out what he was saying, he nodded at my drink and said, "Don't depend too much on that." Then he turned to Sophie who had put her head around the door to call him to the phone.

A roof over my head? Ah yes, the stables where I carve my little

works of art. There are many of them now. I have lined them up
on every available shelf and worktop. Their uniformity is con-
summate; every face, every head and shoulders, every hand, is
identical. In the days, between working and eating, I spend my
time whittling and drinking. When day is over, in the amber light
of turf-fires, in the pale light of moontime, I carve my life away;
I drown it in the golden ambience of whisky no longer watered,
but strong enough to toss cabers. It fills my heart with the blended horrors that night-time brings. So I go to bed, and zoom-time
comes. In the zoom-light of night I see Olive.

Olive with the hazel eyes and short, blonde hair. Her hand
touched that crimson napkin again. She leaned forward on the
table. In the zoom-lens of love, the distance between us collapsed in on itself. Plates and cutlery got swallowed up by some
mysterious black hole. The gap between our worlds diminished.
The white tablecloth, the red candles, the maroon wallpaper, the
gilded light-fittings on the wall, all ceased to exist. The restaurant receded to nothingness. My life, my hopes and dreams,
were filled with Olive. Nothing *was* except her. In that glorious
moment I lived years of knowing her and growing to love her.
She looked stunning, a monument to beauty true and everlast-
ing. She leaned across, her crimson lips parted. She said, "Joe,
you're my dearest friend, *but...*"

Her face receded. Candles blew out, light-fittings popped,
dinner-plates cracked and shattered. Gracious to the end, I paid
the bill and helped her into her coat. The *maitre d'* looked at me
with a pitiable gaze. I was carless, my ex-wife got it as part of
the settlement, so I told Olive I'd hitch. She offered me a lift in
her little red *Yaris*. Even the carpark attendant knew I was jilt-
ed. He shook his head when he saw me in the passenger seat.
Five never-ending minutes limped by. We arrived at a junction
where she stopped to let me out. Dutybound to give me a lift, she
now felt it had been a mistake to offer to take me home. I knew
she wouldn't drive me to my flat in Greystones. She needed to

get away from me, I could see that clearly. She even said so, yet little embers of hope still flickered in my heart. I made one final effort to win her. Wiping away a tear, she gave me that pleading look. In her eyes I saw no face of mine reflected, only the faces of her husband and her children glaring out. Then I knew I was utterly defeated. I stood at the junction for an hour without hitching. I stared at the road she drove down and every time a car came around that corner it was a red *Yaris*. The rain came and I walked all the miserable way to my Greystones flat. Six miles later it was 3am. Too tired, too depressed, too soaked to the skin, I forgot to set the alarm. Next morning I failed to report for work.

So began my slippery slide to Skid Row. Greystones is aptly named; its pallid environs matched the grim interior of my flat. The little love-nest I had hoped to set up for Olive and me soon became a squalid bed-sit littered with the empties and take-aways of a life gone off the rails. For a time I sought refuge in my work; my pupils were good to me as we buried ourselves in maths. Children understand and appreciate a teacher who immerses himself in his work, but parents complained that I wasn't in often enough. Days were lost to hangovers. Then I found the ideal cure for them - drink - so I missed more days. Oftentimes I made an effort to come in for classes but it was hard to negotiate the half-hour bus-ride home without being flashed at by the whisky-peddling publicans who lined my route. So my next day's work was ensnared in a vicious circle, and I was trapped right in the middle.

Even the pubs of Greystones became dark, unwelcoming places. It was my own fault: I sat in a bar one day, immersed in my own misery. The television was too loud; some chatshow host ranted on in that cloying, patronising manner that seems to guarantee a huge salary. It made my blood boil to listen to him, the epitome of modern junk-society. His agenda was simple: stoke 'em up, exploit 'em, leave 'em baying for more. I thought of what this mass info-dump culture was doing to the world. I thought most of all of what it was doing to the children in my school, turning them into little walkman-educated monsters; dissatisfied cynics way before their time, unable to listen to anything for more than two minutes. When I thought of that I could stand it no longer - I chucked a bottle at the TV. The publican disagreed with my censorship and threw me out.

Word soon spread among the pubs. When they saw me in the distance their facades nudged each other and looked the other way. Lounge windows winked slyly, pulling down the blinds when I drew near. Neon signs switched off automatically in a universal show of disapproval. Doors slammed in my face. Snubbed, I sought the comfort of nature. Hours I spent on the beach. Amid the howling wind and breaking waves, amid detritus scattered all around, I contemplated a solution which would have been quick, cold and final. That takes bravery of a kind I never had. There was a half-empty naggin back at the flat - shame to waste it.

Working days became scarce as prime numbers. Whenever I did report in I spent my breaktimes alone in the woodwork room. I found whittling therapeutic and wondered why I had not taken it up before. As I whittled, I thought my life an un-coordinated geometry of problems unsolved, formulae that failed, equations that were anything but simple. I thought too of Olive. Two years I had known her. I thought of how much I loved her. Eighteen months earlier, on a departmental course in the sunny southeast, I had felt the first beats of love in my head. That surprised me. I had not thought of Olive in that way previously. I dismissed the love-notion with the thought of how easy it is to fall for someone in summertime, away from Dublin, away from reality. Six months later, in the middle of winter, I met her for drinks. Love-beats resounded, zoom-time. This was no summer vacation; this was reality on a cold, dirty, mist-soaked night in Dublin. In the year that followed we became the best of friends. Only friends. That didn't stop four or five people in the rumour-factory where I worked from making snide remarks about Olive and me. I dismissed their gossip-mongering with the contempt it deserved, hoping all the time that Olive would someday open up her heart and soul to me. She would not: hubby and the children came first. I gambled all one night in a high-class restaurant. Like the gambler at the gates of Hell, I lost everything... I whittled on through wet-veiled eyes. I thought of how my life was going downhill. I had whittled away Olive, whittled away my wife, my children, my money, my job. When I thought of all these things the knife slipped, my hand bled...

Something else gave too, not just the vein in my hand. Enraged at the injustice of it all, I made straight for the staff-room door and flung it wide open. I stood like a stranger in a pub full of rednecks. Silence descended. My gaze wandered around the room. They all avoided eye-contact; they didn't even notice the little blade in my blood-stained hand. I saw them then for what they were - spineless; I saw what I would be within a week - forgotten; I saw the rumour-mongers, what mileage they would have now. I thought of Olive, sweet Olive - how they had spun their empty gossip with no justification. Three mongers sat by the window, no doubt contriving some new diversion to fill their vacuous lives. One of them saw the knife in my hand. The look of horror that came over her almost made all my misfortunes worthwhile. Just before her contorted mouth broke into a scream, I sent a great glob of spit flying in her direction, turned on my heels, slammed the door behind me, and returned to the woodwork room. Five minutes later the secretary instructed me to attend at the principal's office. "Tell him to go fuck himself," I snapped, and stormed out of the school, never to return. Less than a week later, rather than fritter away my remaining money on a month's rent in Greystones, I took the boat to Holyhead and began my life on the road.

My stars had turned to dust. Failure to solve and graph the inequalities of my life haunted me those first few months. My ratio was out of proportion; there were no magic logarithims to cure the invariables that had unhinged me. Toxins ruled everywhere: the toxins of the material world released toxins in my head. I knew that to rid the psychotoxins from my brain I would have to find somewhere far removed from the frenetic hyperbole of the modern world. If such a place existed, it might be in Scotland.

It was; the major gave it to me.

So I did my odd jobs while increasingly viewing the world through the opacity of a whisky-glass. I whittled a little here, dabbed a little paint there. My stable soon became a treasure trove of hand-carvings, enough to turn the greatest museum green with envy. More than fifty carvings adorned the stable, all identically crafted, identically painted. I sat back admiring them, wondering how many more could fit in one small room... The knock on the door startled me so much I nearly dropped my glass. I put the drink on the table and opened the door. The major stood there for the first time since that fateful night when he had picked me up in his Range Rover. Panic swilled around my malt-ridden stomach. How would he react to the sight of my precious carvings? I heard myself say, "Major Dobbs. Won't you come in?"

He obviously read my defensive body-language. "No thanks, Joe. I have a proposition for you, if you're interested."

Relaxing somewhat, I closed the door behind me. The major was on the tree-lined path that led to the manor. He stood nonchalantly, hands clasped behind his back. I could almost see him in his uniform, a platoon of men listening respectfully and obediently. Behind him, buried among elms and oaks, the sprouting heads of daffodils were showing their yellow faces to the world. "Joe, you know that Sophie, my niece, is very interested in horses, don't you?"

I nodded, dreading what he might say.

"She wants to turn this place into an equestrian centre. She'll need the stables for accommodation."

Nothing lasts forever. I shifted my weight from one foot to the other. Something about a proposition had me puzzled. "You want me to move out?" I said.

"Out of the stables? Yes, but we'll still need someone to do odd jobs. In fact, there'll probably be more jobs now so I may be able to increase your wages slightly. Would the annex behind the garage suit?"

"...Yes... Of course, I-"

"Good. That's settled. There are two conditions."

He wouldn't have noticed me swallowing hard behind my beard.

"You're a good worker despite your problems. You'd be even better sober. Now..." He took his hands from behind his back. In one of them I saw a book covered neatly with brown paper. "Sophie's asked around. A number of her schoolmates could do with some extra help. The money is good for private lessons - say thirty an hour." I could see it clearly now, a maths book. "One of the conditions is that you're not to have touched a drop on any day you're giving tuition. Understood?"

I nodded.

"The other condition is that if you're unwilling to help these children I'll have to let you go. Is that clear?"

I could see the men listening to him alright - more like a whole division than a platoon. "Yes," I said as he thrust the book into my hand.

"That will give you an idea of the syllabus. Be at the manor by ten fifteen tomorrow morning. Your first private tuition is in Edinburgh at eleven thirty." He was on his way up the path before I could even think of synchronising watches.

I closed the door firmly. A dose of the shakes came on me, not entirely from alcohol. I opened the textbook randomly. My eyes fell on a problem about opposite angles in a cyclic quadrilateral. Christ, for a second I wasn't sure how to solve it.

I drank the major's health that evening, then went to bed

early and waited for it to come, the dark, dark zoom-time of the soul. The trigonometry of my mind led me in many directions that night. All the roads I had travelled I walked again. All the people I had met I saw again; those I had damaged and those who had damaged me. In the deep DT's an army of carvings came marching. They had me surrounded. I saw the televisions of Greystones, the meths drinkers of Bradford, the rumour-mongers of Dublin, the whores of Leeds. Hell is a lay-by; Hell is a hotel skip; a meths-soaked rubblesite; a vision at the end of a bottle. Hell is wherever you want to find it, in whatever shape or form you need it. I saw Olive, I saw my children. In zoom-time I cried out. In real-time my body tossed and turned, my hands pulled and tore the sheets. I woke up many times only to die many times. I killed my children and they in turn killed me.

Next day I went to Edinburgh and earned thirty tax-free sterling pounds. I couldn't resist a drink afterwards to celebrate. Now I give six grinds a week, spread over three days. I send half those earnings to Sheila, James and Robbie - they each in turn get their share in the post. I send their mother the amount she deserves - nothing. Robbie will be going to college later this year. I'm thinking of asking him over in the summer. There's no way I can bring myself to return to Ireland, even to see my children. They'll have to use the spare room in the annex.

I'm still a dipso though I try not to drink now before five o'clock. Nights are more tranquil compared to before. My mind still zooms in and out like an accordion on speed, but sleep comes more quickly. I tend not to see people's thoughts and motivations with all the psychic clarity that whisky bestowed on me. Maybe it wasn't the whisky at all. Perhaps it was something deeper that made me view them so judgementally. Whatever it was, zoom-time is less frequent and less intense. For that I give thanks.

Beer is my new tipple. It's easier on the gut. The major's been urging me to attend AA meetings in Edinburgh. I might, I just might. I owe everything to Major Dobbs. Why he put up with me I do not know. Come Christmas-time he and I might have another conversation by the tree. With a bit of subtle persuasion I might get an insight as to why he picked me up out of the gutter. Deep down I think I know why: I got lucky, that's all.

It's peaceful here in the summer. The trees and the firth form a barrier through which the rabble-babble of the brave new millennium does not yet penetrate. There's enough work on the manor now to keep me more than busy. In my spare time I whittle horse's heads for Sophie's new riding centre. As for my other carvings, I did fifty-three of them before finally whittling them out of my soul. Craft shops in Fife and Lothian have been kind enough to take them on a sale-or-return basis, priced £39.99 - I get to keep 70%. Sales have been good so far. They'll probably sell out come the tourist season. Some shopkeepers reckon my carvings go well because of the beauty of the face and the short, blonde hair. Others think it's the crimson napkin that does the trick; the way it matches her lipstick, the way she holds it in her hand. To a man, and woman, they all believe she's raising the napkin to wipe away a tear. Only I know she's lifting it to dab a trace of chocolate sauce from her lips.

NEEDS WANT AS NEEDS MUST

Trains to Happiness depart once in a lifetime, if you're lucky. The one that Cynthia and I boarded was a real slow mover. Our destination was far, far away. First stop Divorce - two stops, actually. Hers and mine.

Cynthia needed weeks to sort out her husband and her life. Meantime, I moved out to that cottage near Miller's Lake. She visited me a lot but I was often on my own. Sleep never came easy at Miller's. My mind was awash with Cynthia and with giving up my home, my wife, my job. The sleep that did come was fractured and full of dreams. Oftentimes I dreamed of Cynthia. Then other, deadlier, dreams slinked into my mind.

I dreamed of hands, pale and elongated. Hands that drew visions of ships, silver and sleek. I see them now, thin and translucent hands, and ships flying in formation from sun to sun. That's when my mind started to act up.

*   *   *

Somewhere in the present-past I walk into a music shop. Appropriate that it begins with a whirling piece of plastic. Everything whirls now. Time itself, no longer straight, circles like a hungry buzzard.

From the moment the laser picked up the first note I knew I had heard it before. Familiarity meant nothing at first - a song is a song, little has not been sung or played in some shape or form already. Funny that I could never recall hearing anything by that group before. A local guru had deemed it *essential* in his week- ly rock column. It is, was, a hobby of mine, building up a vinyl retrospective on CD.

Now, then, whenever it was that I first listened to it, I could- n't believe my ears. It wasn't just the digital rhythms clanging in my head, it was the lyrics - I knew them, too. Cognizance is one thing, prior knowledge another. It was like kissing a corpse. Forty minutes of chords rattling around my brain, cracking open the seed cases of my memory; drums snaring, rolling me in familiarity; guitars smashing to pieces the certainty that I did not, could not, have heard their riffs before. Vocals ripped my mind with the speed of spurting blood. Words I knew so well I could have written them, without ever having heard them before. Looking out over the waters of Miller's Lake, I slowly shook my head.

Alarm bells jangled two days later, or simultaneously, or before. The newspaper headline rang one bell; the reporter's opening phrases rang two; the main body of the report set off the whole shooting gallery. I had read of it a week or two previ- ously, yet here was this newspaper describing it as if it happened only yesterday, then having the gall to say that it *had* happened yesterday. It's amazing how the mind digs up justification where none exists - a survival mechanism, I read somewhere once. That experience put me off reading, made me feel more like conversation. I phoned Cynthia.

*   *   *

Those who say Cynthia and I cheated don't know what they are talking about. Our paths crossed - no premeditation, no scheming, no setting out to have an affair. Soon we knew we were made for each other. We knew because it's not easy living with someone you cannot relate to any more. It forces you to grow apart, develop new interests, have different friends, lead separate lives outside the home. Once the relationship sinks to that level it's amazing how you can put a barricade around your emotions and live for years with someone you should not be living with at all, until you meet someone you should have been living with all along. That's what happened to Cynthia and I: we simply met.

When Cynthia called around I dug out a bottle of wine. Before putting my hand on it I knew every word on that crummy, over-sized label. One glance confirmed that I must have studied it recently, though I had won it in a raffle more than a year ago and had not looked at it since. At least that part of me which knows what most of me is doing most of the time knew that I had not looked at it since. Then the small-talk started. My conversation with Cynthia was like getting pissed before the bottle was opened. Her every word, breath, sigh, action, reaction, blink, gesture, leg-crossing, uncrossing, question, answer, sniffle (she had a cold - I knew that, too, before she did), smile, clearing of throat, pulling of hemline to knee, taking out cigarette, hands clasping, unclasping, laugh, frown... It was like looking at a dove on a distant palm, then a razor-beaked vulture pecks out your eyes. Eventually, Cynthia said something relevant. She said I looked off colour.

I tried to tell her. She put my prior knowledge of the CD down to a misunderstanding. It must have been the re-release of something I had listened to way back at some stoned-out, boozed-out, brain-ossifying party. It had curled up in a remote corner of my mind only to re-surface years later. But I had checked it out. It was a new release. The newspaper she reckoned was some kind of mental quantum leap. The human mind is a wonderful thing, she said. We have powers we rarely use, she said. Sometimes eerie things happen, she said. She started to recall psychic experiences of her own. My pre-knowledge of her words and actions had switched off by now. I drank most of the wine, opened some more bottles, obliterating my pain with alcohol.

Morning comes to night. Cynthia gone, wine gone. In my head knowledge, but of what? Memory is what never was, can never be. Time cranks up, shifts a gear, engages, will slip, has re-engaged. Switch on radio. The newscaster is a dinosaur dredging up the past. Live broadcast, dead news. I know it all already. I flick the volume wheel. Radio low, spirit lower, I feel I do not belong. I leave Miller's Lake, drive into town. Streets are same. Buses turn the corner, their numbers known. Pedestrians, cars, their colours predicted, also size, make and model, exact age, at once the past and future. No present now. Life is my private viewing box in an omniplex where everything is a re-run.

I fight it with will, reason, logic. I think of how it started. Words of another song, *there's someone in my head but it's not me.* Getting hard now to concentrate. I go to shrink, lie on his couch, tell him it's not, is, me. His words soothe me, sleep me...

...white light, yes. A low hum, yes. In the night, dream. Night's dream comes again. Door opening. Stretcher - silver, hovering. Shapes, forms, humans. Humanoid? Yes, no, vaguely. Out the door on the trolley-stretcher thing. More lights make pretty patterns on the placid waters of Miller's Lake. Sky, ship, scalpel. I see those dreamlike hands again. They are pale and elongated, thin and translucent. The hands of a surgeon. They hover over my head. Stretch of skin, incision, cold, slit, scream. Forehead burning, chalk-scrapes shrieking in my head.

Something slithers on steel. Is it steel? Maybe. Cold and clinical certainly. Down, in. I see it slithering, feel it slithering, pushing my brain to one side. It snakes, slinks, sneaks, sidles into my mind. Scalpel, ship sky. Night, door, bedroom. Dream, sleep, wake.

It sleeps in my brain.

Books, TV, internet. I read absorb, regurgitate, and spit out. Behind the shrink's wiry glasses, behind his miserable, money-grabbing eyes, I see paranoid schizophrenia. He is wrong. I hope and pray he is wrong. I tell him he is wrong. He pockets a gold watch paid for by a dozen hypnotic sessions, and looks at me with all the professional pity he can muster.

I get in touch with groups who claim to have been contacted. Weirdos, weirdos one and all. My shelves become littered with abduction stories. Every night I dream of sleek ships hurtling through space and time.

The pressure, I guess, of so many changes in my life. One way of coping with pressure is to dream crazy dreams. That's what Cynthia put it down to, stress. Cutting myself off from my wife, quitting at work, finding the new job, moving to the Lake, waiting while Cynthia sorted out her side of things. The webs we adults must untangle. It was all too much and had manifested itself in disrupted sleep patterns, nightmarish visions. That's what she said. Cynthia was always decisive and clear in her thinking. It was a trait I found attractive. Her quick-wittedness was tested when I told her my theory.

I got as far as the ship over the Lake and the alien presence in my head. I had wanted to explain to her that aliens would never experiment with someone who leads a full and normal life. It would be too easy for friends and relatives to notice unusual shifts in behaviour. Better to scout around for someone going through profound changes. A loner, for instance. Someone living in a remote spot like Miller's. I had wanted to show her that by cutting myself off from my previous existence

I was making myself a perfect target for alien experimentation. Living alone, no longer with a network of friends and family to cross reference my old personality with the emerging one, I was the ideal victim. It was logic, I said. Cold, clear, alien logic.

I never got beyond a sentence or two. In Cynthia's eyes I saw again the pitying look of the wiry-eyed shrink. In her face I saw doubt. I could not risk losing her. She was all I had.

I saw all that she was and all that she meant. Months of knowing flashed by, months that led to the night our hearts touched. The night we tore away the cloak of friendship and saw beneath a beauty raw and deep. Promise we piled upon promise. We cut a channel through the clinging mud of our lives and nothing was ever the same. I saw her childhood, her youth, her dreams, her hopes, shattered by the shackles of other men. In her I saw a mirror that told no lies. We vowed to change it all, to turn the world upside down, to begin again.

Letter of resignation, job application. Lawyers. Her things, my things. Mediation yes, conciliation no. Find a place. Interview. This is my carving knife, this is yours. Job offer, cut in salary, not much to live on. Cut off in-laws. Who gets the car? We can work it out. Avoid mutual acquaintances, start from scratch, change your life, sort it out.

It's so simple.

I love to dream. I have never wanted to be me. Never. Not since looking out over the side of my cot - it's such a long way down.

I remember it all.

First kiss, first smoke, the schoolyard fight, wet dreams, skinny-dipping, the Brady Bunch, guilt, fear, pleasure, Cynthia. Protest marching, Santa outside my window, autumn fruits, snowball fights, sunsets of Java, suffering, people I hate, people I love, Cynthia. Harmony, pain, Mexico, Sunday service, Daddy please don't, jetlag, loneliness, Cynthia. Raindrops, Mummy in the bath with Uncle Henry, the Dakota Building, work, Susan behind the fire escape, Granny dead, Jamie's face pockmarked with sores. Death, politics...

...I re-run it again, live it again, do it again. No memories left; can't tell the difference between pain and panacea. Seepage drains my brain. Myself returns. I will call Cynthia. Must tell her that another presence dwells in my head. Tell her all this time; how it wheedles into my mind, how it sees the future, has lived the present, will live the past. Yes, I will call Cynthia.

She walked in.

"Gordon, you look dreadful. Why are you looking at me like th-"

I see her new, untouched, unseen. Memory mounts reality. I push, pull, rip. Summer frock tears easily. What exactly is summer? I do not, will not, care. Must find out, must examine, must... Hand on mouth, will not scream. Seed of a different reality, a new dimension, can, must, needs. Cross universe. Infiltrate. Will colonise. Has crossbred.

The sweetest memory of all came then - the night she and I declared love. Cynthia smiles. I can tell that from her voice. Voice is everything. The world is a voice in my ear, Cynthia's voice. I lifted the phone not knowing what to say. I had never phoned her without reason, without excuse. I could stand it no longer. Alone too, as I knew she would be, she lifted her receiver on the other side of town and at once drew near. Knowing not what to say, we spoke for more than an hour. Nothing serious, nothing overt - we were both too vulnerable, especially Cynthia. Her marriage had been painful. She did not want to get hurt again.

Darkness claimed the room. Vision faded. My touch surrendered to the body hug of an easy chair. Smell and taste ceased to be. All my senses went to my ears, where her voice filled me. Her gentle lips, her sweet tongue, reached down miles of cable and licked and sucked and probed me to the quick. Past my ear lobes she went, down to my brain, my heart, my scrotum. Yet our conversation was pure as only that of true lovers can be. After ninety minutes on the phone I finally told Cynthia that I loved her; that I had to see her. No, she said, it's not time. Yes, I said, it is. I drove on squealing tyres down all the highways of the world. They all led to her door.

I loved Cynthia then. That was the night we piled hands on hands, hearts on hearts, promises on promises. I loved her eagerly for her sweetness, her sensitivity, her sense of humour, her willingness to always tell the truth as she saw it, to go out of her way to help people, to see the other point of view. Her wholeness, her spontaneity, her belief in what was morally right, her sensuality, her strength in adversity, her belief in other people's excellence, her friendship, her bossiness, her hopes, her solidarity with the downtrodden, her ability to see through dishonesty, her...

...I saw her wince, I saw her weep. I saw her bleed. I could do nothing to stop myself. From somewhere inside my head I watched helplessly as my brute body crushed between us all trust, belief, hope and love. The finest thing I had found in my life - the only thing to focus the future, justify the past, give foundation to the present - I took it between my fingers and crumpled it like gutter garbage. I wanted to shut my eyes to the horror. They would not shut. I wanted to close my ears to Cynthia's pleas. They would not close. I wanted to die. My body would not lie down. I betrayed her, defiled her. Though my actions were beyond my control, my conscience was not. Like an onlooker at the gates of hell, I felt my heart squeezed and constricted by such grief that I could find no way of expressing myself, no way of countenancing my loss.

She lies on bed, crying. Console with tenderness. Yes, tenderness. Pushes me to one side, up on feet, sobbing, grabbing scraps of clothing. She looks at me in - disbelief? Anger? Hatred? Not quite. Memory fastforwards, rewinds. Instant play-back. Hurt! Yes, hurt! Shame, too. Let Gordon back in.

"Cynthia... Darling-"

...she runs, door slamming behind her. Careful must.

I feel them slipping now: hours, minutes, seconds. They stiffen in my memory, shifting, sliding, becoming what never were. Time goes limp. Loops and spirals, no longer linear, no longer Einsteinian. Why? Everything knowable is known, memories all. Live, re-live, die. I must die. Pretence, all is. New workplace I must go to. Act, respond, react. All normal, normal is. Shave, shower, dress neatly, eat properly. Overdrive mind, hyperbrain head. Species must survive. Survival all. New, reborn. There is no time. In dimensions far away there is no time. Beyond stars and galaxies and nebular clouds there is nothing but black hole space. Black holes eat my brain. Memory stretches, elongates, gets sucked in. How can a head so overcrowded be so empty, so drained? Everything plays at different speeds, different times, different places. Finally, all is exhausted. Eject, reject. Nothing is. Everything is, but I am fading. Consciousness is, was once, never.

Absorb, inhale, soak up, infiltrate, engage, take in, colonise, suck in, receive, imbibe, draw in, decode, swallow, embrace, penetrate, implant.

But no Cynthia, mistake that.

Learn, learn, learn.

EVERYONE THIS, NOBODY THAT

At first, I found Monica's fetish for hankering attractive. It was an interest she shared with her closest colleague, Trish, at the fashion house where they both worked. In the first weeks I knew her, she and Trish attended two hankerings, both minor. When she asked me to hanker with her - at the mother of them all, an event she had already attended once - I was flabbergasted. More than that, I wondered how I could afford it.

She volunteered to pay. Her career in the fashion business (behind the catwalk, though I believe she had the face and body for a career on it) had little to do with earning money. An old friend of mine, George, once famously called her a Sloan Ranger. I chided him for his outdated terminology, putting his opinion of Monica down to jealousy. So it was that I, a grafter in a retail park computer company, a once proud socialist, found myself sitting in the back seat of a limo, a beautiful woman by my side. In the distance, the theatre beckoned like an iridescent fishing lure spinning ever closer.

"I haven't eaten all day," she said as our car pulled in.

Something in my eyes prompted her to add, "Don't worry, Cal. Nobody eats on Oscar Day. Everyone indulges at the parties afterwards."

Monica did not notice my annoyance. Everyone this, nobody that: that sort of talk gets my hackles up. She failed to notice because she was checking her shoulders for dandruff. Not that she needed to check. She looked stunning. I hoped the pins and boob-tape would hold her in her dress as crosswinds pummeled us on our way out of the car. She waved royally, walking along the red carpet past wedges of fans, wannabees and photographers. None of them paid me any attention, just as well considering how self-conscious I felt. Something my mother used to say floated into my mind; about it being far from this I was reared. She would have made a fuss had she lived long enough to see her son in a monkey suit. I took Monica's hand and led her into the foyer. Security men, recognising who she was coming as, stepped aside to let her past. One of them leaned forward to check the discreet badge in my lapel with a tiny hand-held scanner. I had opted to go as a member of the audience. Us Ordinary Joes had been known to fake our ID.

Once inside, it was all I had expected, and more.

"Can't you feel the speculation?" Monica was breathless. "It's so rife! There are many potential upsets, especially in the four major categories."

I had trouble recalling what exactly the four majors were - a difficulty alien to most attendees, to judge by their relaxed demeanour. I had three categories worked out when Monica nudged my elbow, pointing with her eyes to a suave-looking man walking through the door.

"Know who he is?"

The likeness was remarkable, the pencil-thin mustache a giveaway.

"Frankly, my dear," I guided Monica to a wine waiter, "I don't give a damn."

One of the few movie quotes I know brought a smile to her face as we sipped two flutes of bubbly. The smile stayed with her, not because of Clark Gable, but because we stood awhile drinking in the atmosphere. She was with the beautiful people, in their most perfect habitat on her night of nights, and she was the most beautiful of all. For a moment I was happy, glad to be part of the latest craze.

"You should have hankered fully, Cal, rather than being just an invited guest."

"Thought I'd dip my toes before jumping in."

"To hanker properly you have to be someone else, not a member of the audience. You should have come as your favourite actor. I would have paid for it."

I grunted and counted the bubbles in my glass.

"Nobody's wearing anything outrageous this year. Thank goodness for that."

"Restraint must be this year's theme," I said.

She gave me that funny look. But she was right. Nothing was over the top. If anything, hers was the most revealing dress. It stopped just short of being gauche, and was attracting some attention, especially from a few older men standing nearby.

"Barbra!"

"Juliette. Darling!"

I turned. Trish came swanning across the floor, larger than life. From her beehive hairstyle it was obvious which Barbra she had opted for, but Monica?

"Juliette?" I ventured. "You mean Julia Rob-"

"Oh my God!" Trish gasped as she caught Monica by the hand, nearly spilling her champagne.

"I can't take him anywhere," hissed Monica. "He didn't want

me to tell. He wanted to guess."

Now that I'd made an ass of myself, I decided to ham it up. "You mean you're not here as Julia Roberts?"

"Oh my God!"

Trish's repetition was becoming tiresome. Monica leaned toward me and explained, "Juliette Binoche, winner of best supporting actress for *The English Patient*. Nominated, but did not win, for *Chocolat*."

I hid behind my champage glass again and let them chat. Thankfully, it was time to take our seats. "Juliette?" I offered her an arm to link with. That brought her smile back, though not as effusively as before.

We had barely warmed our seats when she said, "We're in the right part of the auditorium, not up there with the cheapo's."

I craned my neck. With an orbital sweep my eyes took in the balcony and the high, imposing ceiling. "Impressive," I said, finding myself spellbound by the ultimate theatre of dreams.

"Recognise anyone?"

I looked around. On the other side of the central aisle, not far from Barbra Streisand, an unmistakable Marilyn Monroe.

"Lookalikes are obvious, Cal. They go as the same person each time. Others are more difficult. There, third row back, five seats in from the left. Who's that man?"

Also audience gazing, he had turned in our direction. I studied him hard but his face was a mystery to me.

"It's not fair to ask who he is when you haven't heard his voice. I heard him speak last time. Very posh."

My face remained blank as an Oscar statuette.

"Richard Burton, stupid. Nominated seven times, never successful. That's the most ever nominations without a win, a record he shares with Peter O Toole."

Monica's encyclopedic knowledge did not faze me, though the presence of a seven-times nominee worried me in a different way. "How long will this go on for... Juliette?"

"Three hours - half an hour less than the historic Academy Awards. There are fewer technical gongs, apart from costume design, and none of the nerdy stuff like Best Sound Editing or Best Live Action Short. Has to be like that, with so many multiple nominees."

Absence of technical awards cheered me, though the prospect of each nominee having all nominations listed did not. Juliette's category, Best Supporting Actress, contained thirteen nominations - her two plus eleven between the three other nominees. This meant her odds of winning were 13/2, longer than at the traditional Oscars. Experience, in the form of her chagrin, had taught me never to refer to the traditional Oscars as *real*, but to always use a euphemism such as her own personal favourite: *historic*.

Juliette was not successful this time. She took it well, having told me beforehand that the selection committee was notoriously biased toward big names. When a multiple winner like Katherine Hepburn turns up in your category, chances are she'll win again. Though it didn't always happen like that. This was the excitement of it, she said, not knowing whose turn it might be. That and the thrill of seeing your face burned in on the nomination clips on the big screen.

The evening went well. Steve Martin played a host of devastating wit. Instead of tacky dance routines, we were treated to a number of tight, tasteful songs by impersonators of the highest calibre. The speeches, which I had been dreading, were remarkably restrained. Nobody threw a Paltrow or a Berry. Winners untimely enough to stray beyond their allotted thirty seconds were drowned out by the orchestra. The half minute rule did have one entertaining side-effect: everyone spoke very fast.

The mechanics of the ceremony seemed clear when Monica explained them to me. The nominee's age was irrelevant. Portray them in their twenties, or depending on your years, impersonate them at the end of their careers. At an interlude

Monica showed me a photo of Binoche. She resembled her in many ways and was the correct age, yet it was uncanny how many of the non-lookalike nominees adopted the mannerisms and persona of their subjects. Take Judy Garland. I recognised her through a combination of garish make-up and a bottle protruding from her handbag. Her companion, young enough to be a daughter, had short black hair. Their relationship seemed rather tetchy if their demeanour at our *après*-ceremony table was anything to go by.

"Don't worry," Juliette reassured me with a whisper. "Those two are always like that. Judy had to be content with an honorary Oscar. She's never forgiven her daughter for winning the real thing."

A rare silence fell on Judy Garland, Barbra Streisand, Juliette, and the four others sharing our table. I chose that moment to lead the conversation. "I must say, Lisa, that was one great performance in *Cabaret*. Did you win an Oscar for that role?"

Her doe-like eyes expanded like gas balloons. Her ruby lips pursed. She looked away. So did everyone else at our table, except Garland, who slugged back her gin and banged her glass on the table. With an overdone glint in her eye, she laughed: "Guess you're not well up in the knowledge department, honey. *Cabaret* got eight Awards. Of course Little Missy here walked away with a gong."

"It's okay for not knowing," her daughter glared at me. "Not everyone is an expert."

"At least nobody did a Brando tonight," Juliette said, quickly.

I thought better of digging more holes and let them chatter on without me. Juliette seemed ashamed to look my way, preferring the animated conversation of Barbra Streisand's companion, a man by the name of Jeff. Probably Goldblum, one of the few celluloid faces I could put a name to, though something about this Jeff did not seem right. Between the champagne and the whisky I was getting beyond caring. I let my attention wander to the exotic people at other tables, lit up as they were in the stark spotlight of this crazy, twisted reality.

My eyes did my thinking. The men looked like they had been cast in bronze. It was a wonder they were not hunched over by the weight of their jewellery and their puffed-up wallets. Some were unspeakably wealthy, so many Tom Hanks's and John Fords shelling out small fortunes to have a better chance of winning. The current rate ranged from two grand to be in the audience up to fifty for impersonating Walt Disney - or Bob Hope, who had presented the historic Oscars thirteen times (hosting was allocated not by the committee, but by lottery).

I wondered how many hundred speeches would go unheard. These were not my kind of people, these hankerers. To them it scarcely mattered that their Oscars did not have eight hundred million viewers, nor that this was not the real theatre, but a phony one, dressed, like them, to kill. What counted was the peer kudos of being there. It must have cost Monica twenty grand for both of us. She still chatted to Jeff, and looked very happy. It wasn't her beauty that drew my eyes. An aura surrounded her, a radiance from somewhere - possibly just from being here. Other women had it, too. Their beauty stopped my breath. Indigo was obviously the new black, if their dresses were anything to go by. As for the flesh, I had never seen such tanning, styling, dieting, buffing, preening, plucking... So much effort to look so fabulous. A lady at the next table drew my gaze, so attractive was she in an effortless kind of way. I heard her name and turned to Juliette, hoping to drag her attention away from Goldblum.

"Look. That's Lauren Bacall at that other table."

"I know." Juliette shrugged. "I spoke to her last time. She's a loser, famous for being the hottest favourite never to have won an Oscar. Some people like being losers. Sad, really."

Her dismissive tone fazed me. I turned to look at Bacall

again. Juliette's voice whispered in my ear: "*The Mirror Has Two Faces* was the Academy's last chance to honour her after her long career. Biggest shock in Hollywood history when the envelope for Best Supporting Actress was opened and they chose not to award it. Gave it to me instead," she grinned.

I knew nothing about *The Mirror Has Two Faces*. What I did know was that I was staring at the Bacall of *To Have And Have Not*. I watched her shake her wavy blonde mane and stub out a cigarette. I read her sultry lips as she asked those at her table, "Anybody got a match?" A man of middling age handed her a book of matches. I wondered if there was a huskiness to her voice and tried to make sense of what Juliette had said about losers. Something in Bacall's character, that strange fusion of hard sex and open vulnerability, made me think that the only people here that I could get on with *were* losers... Seemed ironic to me that Bacall had been pipped by my girlfriend. It started me thinking that perhaps there was a lesson in this somewhere.

I knew I was getting maudlin. I turned my shoulder on Lauren Bacall and tried to mingle at my own table. I tapped Juliette's arm to get her attention, so engrossed was she in whatever Jeff Goldblum was saying.

"Darling," she said, "Jeff's been telling the funniest jokes!"

She asked him to repeat them. I listened. Whatever humour the man had was lost on me, but in his telling I noticed familiarities, like the set of his jaw, a certain jerkiness to his head movements. Then I realised who the joke-teller was. It was not Goldblum at all.

Starman had come back down to Earth and was telling a Polish joke.

We finally jettisoned Jeff Bridges at four in the morning at a taxi rank. Monica seemed reluctant to let him go. She was not talkative in the cab except to remind me: "Don't call me that. Say Juliette."

I did, especially in bed, hoping it might arouse her. She flicked my hand away with a sullen, "You nearly ruined the whole night. We were with stars from every era and you fucked everything up."

"I'm sorry," I muttered, moving over to the cold part of the sheet.

Next day Monica looked me bitterly in the eye. "Time we stopped playing games, Cal. You and I are growing apart. You better go. We both need the distance."

Who was I to argue? The sleepless space of the previous night had brought it home to me that we were not suited. She had obviously been thinking the same thing.

"Goodbye... Juliette." I stood beside my car and it crammed with all my belongings.

Wordlessly, she stepped back and closed the door of her townhouse behind her.

My good friend George and his wife Rhia took me in for a few days to tide me over until I could find a place of my own. During my first night there, after too many malts, I confided to George that he been right to call Monica a Sloan Ranger, though I still berated him for his out-dated terminology. On my second night, after an unsuccessful day spent flat-hunting, I glimpsed several issues of *Hankerer, Inc* in their magazine rack. When I scoffed at hankering - typical me, I couldn't keep it in - they seemed preoccupied for the rest of the evening. George wouldn't even come to the pub that night, very unusual for him. "Go out yourself," he said, and I did.

Next day I found a comfortable flat not far from work. I moved in the same evening, conscious that I had overstayed my welcome with George and Rhia. That night, sorting through my stuff, I found three of Monica's CD's in among box-loads of my own. Next morning I put them in the glove compartment, making a mental note to drop them at her place whenever I might pass by.

Hankering was gaining a hold on my colleagues at the computer company, too. They could talk of little else. It scared me the way it was becoming very incorrect to question it. It seemed like a grip, a noose, was tightening, encompassing everyone. Scepticism like mine was increasingly no longer an option.

One week after moving into my flat, a business call brought me within sight of Monica's road. Rush-hour traffic was painful so I pulled in to a convenient parking spot. I thought about dropping the discs through her letterbox but changed my mind and rang the doorbell. At five in the afternoon I figured she'd be in.

"Cal!"

"Hello, Monnie."

For a moment she looked startled. Other than that she seemed okay. Her hair was the way I remembered it from the Oscars. Though her dress was different, it exuded the same sense of glamour as the creation she had worn on our last night. Strange clothing to wear, I thought, at this time of the day. In the doorstep exchange that followed, the obligatory *How-have-you-been-keeping?* leading to the compulsory *Fine*, I began to sense something from her, an air that was not real, not right. Ignoring it, I waved the CD's under her nose. "Thought you might want these."

"Y-yes. Actually, I found something belonging to you. Your box of brushes and paints."

I hadn't dabbled in watercolour for months, and only then recalled putting the painting set behind her piano.

"Wait here." She half closed the door on me, forgetting the discs.

I forgot about them too, until I saw them in my hand and decided to follow her in. Old longings haunted me down her hallway, as far as the sitting room. The longing stopped when she heard me walking in. She turned from the piano, a panicky look rooting across her face.

"Hello Cal."

One glance at the hard set of the jaw, the jerky flick of the head, and I knew who it was.

"Em, do you remember Jeff?"

Of course I remembered him.

"Juliette's been telling me about you."

He was walking toward me, hand outstretched. *Greetings, Earthling.*

"Juliette? You mean Monica. You're not still playing that game, are you, Monnie?"

In the periphery of my eye, the coffee table was strewn with celebrity mags, fashion glossies, and the latest hankering guides. More of them than when I'd lived here. I noticed one of the celebrity-surgery supplements that came with the latest issues.

"Cal, everyone's doing it. Nobody sees any harm in it."

There she went again. Everyone this, nobody that. Something snapped.

"What are you up for now?" My voice was harsh, loud, almost a shout. "A Bafta? A Brit?"

"Cal. You don't understand-"

"-A Tony? A Grammy?"

"It's all the rage, Cal. Everyone's doing it. It's uncool not to."

"That's all you care about, isn't it? Image. Surface. Gloss. Nothing else matters. This is pathetic!" A sweep of my hand took in all of her magazines and guides.

"I think you'd better go." *Starman* stepped closer, finger-pointing at me, then at the door.

"Jeff, don't." With one hand she held him back and with the other shoved the art box at my chest.

"He's not Jeff Bridges, and you're not Juliette Binoche!"

"Just go." She rammed the art box further into my chest.

I took it in my hands and turned on my heels. As a parting shot I couldn't resist, "And the Oscar goes to... Jeff Bridges, the fastest mover in all of Tinseltown."

I heard her hold him back again, her voice rattling down the hallway. "Get out!" she shrieked. "Get out!"

Work kept me sane for more than a fortnight. Even in the busiest periods Monica was never far from my thoughts. Night after night I sat in my lonely flat, head and heart bursting with empty feelings. I felt like a religious nut losing his faith. It was for the best that we had split yet it pained me to think her mind was blotted out by this caricature of a lifestyle - a dreamy, insubstantial lifestyle fostered by dozens of hanker guides and agencies springing up like jungle shoots. The growing popularity of hanker-surgery was something I could not tolerate. The experience I had gone through with Monnie and her phony celebrity-identity left me with no desire to meet other people. Hankering was happening all over town. I sought escape in music and the occasional documentary.

There were nights when the sun slipped too quickly below the city skyline, when there was nothing on the channels and I had no ears for music. I would go to bed early, waiting for darkness to come, to release me from the zillion what-ifs flitting in my head. I convinced myself that I was working so hard I needed extra sleep. One of those nights someone rang my flat-bell. I scrambled out of bed and hobbled downstairs. No silhouette in the porch. Cautiously, I opened the door and looked out. No one. A shiver came from somewhere, resonating through me in the mild autumn night. A cat screamed in the distance. Something moved behind me. I swivelled. She was standing right behind me.

"Time to get blanked, Cal."

Her face, the dead set of her eyes, broke on me the coldest sweat.

"People everywhere are getting blanked."

I almost fell backwards down the steps to the pavement. Instinctively I grasped the garden railing to stay upright.

"I know who you can be, Cal."

She was gliding across the porch toward me.

"It won't hurt."

She floated after me as I bolted down the steps. I ran into the street, a fugitive from my own doorstep. City lights towered overhead, bending their arcs to illuminate me, chasing me until I ran so far the city faded with every stride. Cover of darkness was no use. She still followed, a ghost gliding on tarmac. Brambles ripped my face as I blundered off the road. I hid out in the woods. Wolves howled, rain pelted me. My throat ached, so ragged was my breath. Terror stalked the trees, my legs hurt from wild running. Everywhere I looked she was there, circling, watching, waiting. Police lights and helicopters lit up the woods. In the distance I heard the howls of sniffer dogs.

I swam against the tide of a mighty river and nearly drowned. I hauled myself up the far side, heart jumping like a bullfrog, clambered across a ridge and saw a row of houses. I was back where I had started, at the fraying edge of the city. Sprinting again, I hoped to lose her in suburbia. Pains battered my chest but fear kept me going. I turned a corner and ran into a pile of dustbins on the pavement. I tried to hurdle them but the clatter of metal on concrete proved my undoing. The deadly sound of converging sirens had me sprinting again. I tilted full pelt into an alleyway, only just stopping myself from scudding into a brick wall.

I had run into a dead end.

Harsh, gritty breath tore my throat like strips of gravel. My heart wrenched loose from my ribs with every pounding beat. Bent over, unable to stand, legs quivering like tree stumps in an earthquake, I lifted my gaze.

"It's no use, Cal."

She stood at the head of the alley. Her head creaked unnaturally to her left. A man stepped from the shadows.

"Looks like you've captured him at last, Officer," I heard her say.

Sweat dripped from my forehead into my eyes. The gloom of

the alley nearly blinded me. I was nearly collapsing from the chase. Through salty blinks I saw enough to recognise the man standing beside her. There was no mistaking that grin. Self-satisfied, in an understated way.

My favourite actor, Mr Tommy Lee Jones, took a scissors from his pocket and pointed it at me. The scissors forked, silver blades lurching forward, growing large in a cartoonish way. The huge scissors reached across the alley and had me in an instant, pinching my arm tight, pinning it against a brick wall. The blades had expanded so much that Binoche and Jones were each able to take a handle in both their hands. Then I understood. If Tommy Lee Jones was Officer Gerárd, I was the One-Armed Man.

Suddenly sleeveless, I watched the skin on my arm bulge. It turned purple as the icy blades pressed into my naked, tender flesh. I could do nothing but stare at my own amputation. Veins stood like ridges. My bones compacted as silver metal pinched tighter, constricting me in a sharp, steely grip, crushing me like a sausage in a vice. Still my skin held out, though my arm looked like twin balls of blood in balloons of pale, skein-like flesh. I glanced pleadingly at Binoche and Jones. They shoved the handles closer together, gorging on me with their eyes, a crazed look on their faces. I felt then the give of soft flesh. The skin on my arm exploded in a slow-motion way. In my throat I felt a rising scream. My eyes could not leave my arm, so drawn were they to the cutting... Binoche and Jones heard my silent scream. I know they heard it. As blood spurted, my open mouth vented its silence with a shriek so blood-curdling it blew darkness from the alley, illuminating me in a light that was shrill and white, the light of purest pain.

As the scream came I pitched sideways, sweating and shivering in the creamy light of dawn that streamed in through the window of my flat. I sat up in bed, breathing hard. I felt my arm hanging from me, unsevered. I stayed upright like a terrified child, my heart not slowing for minutes. My head tried to come

to terms with the worst nightmare I had ever had. I glanced at
my bedside clock. It was 5.28am.

I turned up for work early, freshly showered, looking almost as
if I'd had a good night's rest. Our receptionist, Nikki, had gone
for the full surgery makeover. There was no mistaking her coy
look as she welcomed me from behind her desk. I noticed my
colleagues waxing on about hankering even more than usual. At
coffee break I saw the poster on the wall and realised why they
were excited. It was not because our receptionist had changed
into Lady Di, but because a staff hankering party was to be held
that night. Everyone would be expected to attend. At lunch time
the boss put his hand on my shoulder. "Who are you coming as,
Cal? Star of music, stage or TV? Some other kind of celebrity?
Do you want to win an Award?"

    "I-I'm not sure yet."

    "Have a look at these." He handed me a bundle of the latest
guides. "Don't be out in the cold. Everybody wants to be there.
Nobody wants to be left out."

During a lull in the office I sifted through the hanker guides,
opened one and slipped it into the hard-drive. I flipped through
the files until I came to a star with a mischievous twinkle in his
eye. For one night only, it said. I put my elbows on the desk and
cupped my chin in my hands. One night only. My own reflection
peered out from behind the portrait on the screen, eerily matching it like a dissolve between two criminal faces in one of those
documentaries about forensics. One night. If I didn't make my
move now somebody else might reserve it. There would be no
availability then until the next day. Maybe just this once. What
harm could there be in just one night? This was the only star for
me. My finger hovered for less than a second before pressing the
button with a tremulous 'yes'.

    It took me a while to download all the tips on favourite sayings, postures, mannerisms, facial expressions. I thought I knew most of them but it's amazing how much homework needs to be done for correct hankering. Surgical makeover was not an option, given the shortage of time, not that I wanted that for a single night. My hair was similar to his both in colour and style. Though my nose was not prominent enough, it was of a size to let me get away with it.

Now that I'd decided to commit, my excitement grew. At lunchtime I phoned a theatrical shop to reserve what I needed. They had it all and were remaining open until six. I wouldn't even have to hurry after work to get there. As afternoon turned to evening I found myself getting on better with my colleagues than I had in months. They seemed friendlier, as if I had suddenly become a team player. I felt happier than I had been in weeks. There seemed a certain karma about the way the day was shaping up, a coming together of things to convince me that my decision to hanker was the right thing to do. The party would be for me a trial run. As the day wore on I even contemplated undergoing surgery if things worked out well that night. Who knows, I might re-introduce myself to Juliette and Jeff... well, Juliette anyway.

At twenty to six I picked up the suit. It fitted perfectly. The glasses were exact replicas. The moustache looked real enough to shave. I spent a few hours learning off my homework before taking a cab to the office party.

I made a grand entrance, brandishing my cigar with an appropriate flourish. Everyone turned to look. The party music faded in one of those heart-stopping cinematic moments. My heart stopped too. What if I had it wrong? Would my own nose look ridiculous? I knew I had got it right when I saw the smile on the boss's face as he stepped toward me. Everyone else smiled too when they saw him lead the way. He spread his arms to welcome me with a bear-like embrace. He took my hand and shook it warmly. "So glad you could make it," he said. "Now, the drinks are on me, Groucho."

Boy With The Shine On His Face

With a sweep of his arm Matt Clifford knocked the folder marked Boy 121 clean off his desk. Scans flew everywhere: CAT and MRI, EEG's and positrons, lists of betablockers, anti-depressants, examination sheets, evaluations. Clifford watched them swish down into silence, the sad testimony of broken dreams.

His cheeks flushed, his palms felt sweaty. He regretted lashing out, the violence of his gesture untypical of the man but he needed to express frustration. Failure was not what he was accustomed to. Scattered files did not matter. They were saved on the hard drives. They did not matter because they had proved useless in the sad circumstances of the boy whose real name was Shane - a name used less and less as case workers referred to him more and more as Boy 121; the Boy with the Shine, the boy with the unique combination of unrelated symptoms which, as Dr Matt Clifford knew, formed a distinct clinical entity, a new syndrome for which no known cure existed.

The file for the first instance stared up at him. Its opening pages opened seductively in the fall to the floor, revealing enough of a glimpse to trigger in Clifford's mind a reconstruction of that toxic day when Shane ran between rows of computer screens that bowed their heads like freakish honour-guards.

The boy caught a glimpse of himself in one of the screens. Streaks of gummed down yellow hair above shiny, puffed-out cheeks and a blurred school shirt. A rush of data reflected on a monitor.

"Slow down, Shane." Moya, computer room assistant, had on her nice tone not her harsh voice. "My, Shane, you're sweating. You've been working too hard staying back helping me tidy up."

Shane slowed but could not resist saying: "I can't stop thinking about my puppies, Moya. I think of them every few minutes!"

The assistant smiled sweetly. Before she could think about asking after the puppies the boy slipped past her and was on his way out the door.

Shane slowed again in the schoolyard. His forehead felt strangely sweaty, like one of those night-fevers Mom made better. He had some kind of headache. It took him longer than usual to locate Rory and Ted. They were at the far end of the playground.

"I've been thinking about my puppies all day!" he yelled at his friends. He would have danced around Rory and Ted had he been feeling better, if only Warren Hunter hadn't appeared there and then and thumped him in the back.

"Hey, leave him alone!"

"Yeah? Make me."

Hunter was twelve, twice as big, three grades ahead, four years older, five times stronger. Shane regained his balance, mind whirling with the diminishing excitement of puppies, the clamminess of whatever he was coming down with, and the sudden arrival of the schoolyard bully.

"I said leave him alone."

"Yeah, leave him alone. We'll tell on you."

Hunter ignored the other boys. "What are you staring at, dipstick?"

Shane's breath congealed like hot treacle in his throat. This was not what playtime was supposed to be. Especially the last playtime before hometime, puppytime. Somewhere in the distance Mr Collins rang the bell for classes to line up. Shane heard the bell swirling like wurlitzers at a fairground. Round and round the horses went, round and round the noisy bell went. Suddenly, he had to bend backwards. Hunter was leaning forward, head bloated like a goldfish in a bowl, pressing into him. "I'm talking to you, tomato-face. I said I'm..."

Hunter pulled back. A strange look came over his face as his voice trailed away. Shane straightened and looked the bully in the eyes. Hunter would be gone after summer but this was May. A whole five weeks of Hunter before the holidays. Five long weeks that stretched like an elastic band.

Like a never-ending stretch of elastic, something had to give.

Dr Clifford had walked across his file-strewn floor to the window of his consultancy. He stared out past his own reflection to the faraway London Eye, beyond that across hundreds of miles to his holiday home in Wales. The cottage near Bala was a different world where he longed to be at times like this. He had bought it with his own money, in his name only, the best move he ever made because Becky could not get her greedy hands on it as part of her divorce settlement.

The one good thing about his former wife was that when she intruded into his mind, she brought on her coat-tails thoughts of his eleven year-old son, Simon. Clifford knew that thinking about Simon was the best way of ridding Becky from his brain, but since he had taken on the case of Boy 121 he found himself haunted by the fear that his own son might turn out like Shane.

At times like that he thought he might even feel sorry for Becky if she ever had to go through what had happened to Shane's mother six weeks after the schoolyard incident.

It had been a day like any other. The monotone chimes of Angelus bells rang out from the Catholic church behind the ivy-clad gable of a big old Victorian red-brick. The house, like Shane's mom, had seen better days.

"Mind the plate. It's hot." She rubbed her hands on the tea-towel she used to carry the plate from the microwave. Shane's face glistened slightly. From play activity, she hoped, or because of glare from the tungsten strip overhead.

Mom put food on the table this time every evening. She had recently insisted on eating her dinner with him as part of a pro-gramme set up jointly by the home-school liaison officer and the local psychology service. It was a strategy Mom could hardly have envisaged two months previously. When she thought about it she blinked hard and bit her lips, forcing herself to listen to the radio. A singer with a rude name was rapping about 'doing it in the shower'. She remembered Shane asking what 'it' was when he first heard that song. It put a lump in her throat to think of it because that was in those innocent days before all this trouble at school.

She peered at him from the corner of her eye. He was pick-ing at his burgers, beans and chips, chewing them more than usual. Good for him. He had been told not to gulp it down like the puppies. She felt deflated then, at the way he seemed to be neglecting the two Yorkies. That trouble at school had distract-ed him so much he could not concentrate on his pets for the last six weeks. His bright blue eyes hidden as he bowed his head to eat his food, his yellow hair like a cornfield after a hailstorm, his face a picture of boyish innocence as in the framed photos on the cabinet behind him.

They were wrong. She looked down and sliced her meat with the knife so close to the fork she heard the scrape of metal above the radio babble. The rapper had finished and the DJ was prattling on in that annoying way of his. They were definitely wrong. Shane was an angel at home. No way could he be what they said he was at school. It was not his fault. He was misunderstood. It was the other children, those teachers... She raised her eyes to look at him again.

The bean hit her left cheekbone with a surprisingly cold splat as though punishing her for not heating it enough. The impact stunned her. She saw another bean on the edge of Shane's plate. His finger was cocked.

"Shane!"

He flicked this one lower, harder. It too veered left, hitting her chest. His face broke up in fits of laughter.

She glanced at the bean stuck in its own saucy aureole, an obscene second nipple on her left breast. It slid slowly down leaving a slimy trail like blood on her lavender blouse.

"Shane. Please!"

He had his eye in now. Beans flew in clumps straight at her. She put up her hands to defend her face, her fingers a mad mixture of saucy beans and salty tears.

"Shane. Stop. Please stop!"

As soon as she took her hands from her face she saw him fling the burger like a frisbee. It hit her square on the bridge of the nose. Her shuddering cry drowned out by his mad squawks, she saw through the tears, the cold sauce, the painfully hot grease, that his face was shiny and as red as the beetroot on her chicken salad.

Clifford looked down at so many manila files strewn across his floor like autumn leaves waiting to be kicked. At the foot of one of the cabinets crouched a photo, that school portrait where Shane's face shone like a fog light. Take away the shiny face, add in the posed uniformity of all school photos, and in that pound-shop frame Clifford glimpsed his own son staring back at him with a face so trusting. Just like the portrait handed to him by Shane's mother at their first meeting.

"It was taken on one of his bad days," she had said, as if Dr Clifford did not know that from the brightness of the shine.

Clifford made a habit of studying parent as much as child at initial interview. There was no father. Dad had skipped the country when Shane was three. Mom was not the strident parent Clifford spent half his life verbal-jousting with. She oozed a soft-spoken fatalism that confirmed the seriousness of the case. A woman at tether's end, and a boy with an alleged persona that seemed at odds with reality.

Shane stood between mother and psychiatrist. He looked bewildered in the saucer-eyed way of a nine-year old. Someone, it must have been himself, had gelled his wavy blond hair so ridiculously to his head it reminded Clifford of beached seaweed on top of a face that was rough and hard-boned like a sports mad kid, yet he had not the slightest interest in games of any kind. Thankfully, his face was pale and dry. He talked freely and quietly, saying 'yes, please' and 'thank you' when Clifford offered an organic cola. Mom excused herself to get coffee, so she said, smiling reassuringly as she walked out through the outer office, past Clifford's console-tapping secretary and the humming printer.

"I know you did a project on Komodo dragons. Are they dangerous?"

"No, unless you're foolish enough to go too close." Shane pronounced the double vowel in 'foolish' with a childish ghostly hoot.

Matt Clifford heard it as the speech pattern of a precocious nine year old. At this first encounter he did not wish to probe too deeply, content to surface-listen for dissident traits.

"They're carnivores but their danger to humans is greatly exaggerated." Shane described their habitat and what they looked like in fine detail, inflecting words like 'carnivore' and 'exaggerated' with childish theatricality. "They're the largest of the lizards, growing to three metres," Shane continued earnestly. "They're very slow-moving, and are endangered like a lot of other species in Indonesia." He paused, swallowed, blinking excessively. "Extinction is a th-thr-threat..." He fingered his neck as if something in his throat was annoying him.

Clifford put the faltering speech down to childish mispronunciation until he noticed how unnaturally sweaty the boy's forehead had become. Shane jutted his jaw, straining his neck beneath the stiff lemon collar of his school shirt. Clifford was unnerved. He saw flashes of a doll's head turning full circle before him, as if Shane's skin had turned to porcelain and a bright light had focused on his face. A bead of glossy sweat fell from the boy's forehead onto the couch. Clifford's eyes followed the droplet. It plopped into the soft fabric. He looked up at the boy's face. Sweat was streaming over a complexion red as raw meat. Shane batted his eyelids, spraying little arcs of persiration. "It's one of my headaches!" he squealed, words pealing from him in a half-whine of desperation. Clifford reached across. The boy backed away, scrabbing with his hands like a frightened puppy. "Fuck off, cocksucker," he yelled. "Fuck off!"

Clifford picked up the scattered files. His back twitched with each scoop of his arm, his shovel-like hands more suited to a labourer than a shrink. Eventually he had the files on his desktop again. Useless reports beginning with the obligatory 'Shane presented himself as a polite and normal...' Clifford detested these rote forms, having no respect for the psychologists who compiled them as though filling in blank spaces in a sentence. His desktop pointed to a maze of blind alleys. Pages of genetics shed no light. Scans were useless. No disorder of the higher brain functions. No inner ear defects. Headaches caused not by muscle contraction. Not by a shutdown of blood supply. Not by fatigue or anxiety. Not by allergy. Not. Not. Not. Nothing positive, plenty negative. Ophthalmoscope examinations: negative. Cerebellum studies: negative. Doses of Ritalin and other heavy sedative drugs: negative. Psychiatric appraisal for schizophrenia: negative. There was even a letter from the mother suggesting spirit possession, also negative. There were plenty of labels: ADD. ADHD. Coin your own, invent a tag - none were adequate.

Matt Clifford felt like thrashing the files to the floor once more and stomping them into the fashionably bare floorboards. Those he had re-read he slammed back onto the desk. His secretary could put them in order. It's what he paid her for. As for the secret file, the one containing the truth, there was never any danger of his secretary stumbling across that because it had yet to be written. But write it he would and present it to his peers. They could go take a hike for all he cared about how it might damage his reputation. If he could convince them, or find some cure for Shane, then his standing would be enhanced. If not, who cared for reputations? It was time for the far-fetched, career-wrecking truth. If it did cost him his job so what? How much was a consultancy worth, no matter how glitzy, how lofted, compared to the well-being of a boy?

The Snowdon Mountain Railway could barely keep pace with the hill walkers, never mind raise enough steam for a decent clickity-clack. That did not bother young Shane, his face grinning with joy as the rain-soaked train pulled into a station house in the clouds.

"We'll walk down if the mist clears," Matt Clifford said when the two of them ventured out of the mountaintop café.

"Beats walking up!" Shane's rain jacket flapped like bat's wings as he jumped in the air, landing with both feet on a flat rock near the cairn of stones marking the summit. As if, on cue, his thudding feet had pressed a secret button in the rocks, the veil of drizzle parted. Like a silver curtain in an old-fashioned cinema, mother nature pulled back her wispy tendrils to reveal a sight that was stunning even for a cynic in his mid-thirties like Dr Matt Clifford.

A mountain lake took their breaths away. It shone up like a faraway mirror reflecting shimmering blue. Rain at their backs now, dissipating clouds revealed more. Far below them a mosaic of pine green valleys. Beneath their feet the slate grey of Snowdon and other mountains that surrounded them but were not so high. On mountain trails climbers the size of ants discarded slickers and oilskins that glistened like flags in crystal light. The full whack of the sun hit them with pure glare. Shane squealed with delight, gleaming from a mixture of wind in his face, cloud vapour and real perspiration, but no shine. He began to peel off his jacket, jumping up and down again.

"Keep it on. It's a few degrees cooler up here."

"Gee - it's *colder* than down there!" Voice full of the discovery of childhood, face lit up with amazement.

"That's Ireland over there."

"Where?"

Matt Clifford pointed to the west. He had heard that sometimes, if conditions were right, people claimed to be able to see that far. He didn't know if it was true or not. It seemed the sort of thing to say to a nine year old.

"Hello Ireland!"

As Shane hollered westward through cupped hands, Matt Clifford's face broke into a grin. The boy *had* been happy for days, no sign of the shine, a bellyful of chocolate doughnuts in his tummy from the summit café, a whole world laid out beneath his feet in this mystical, timeless place that Clifford loved so well. Suddenly he saw his own son in Shane's boots. That made him wonder if Boy 121 was some kind of substitute. Clifford tried to remember the last time he had made Simon as happy as he had made Shane. He resolved to give his son an equally good time, which made him feel guilty. He still smiled bravely.

The shine came then. What caused it to appear came as no startling revelation to the psychiatrist. He could hardly miss the teenager with the blaring radio.

Later that night when Shane had gone to bed in Clifford's holiday home near Bala, the psychiatrist added the radio incident to his growing list of evidence. To convince himself he sat on his patio and stared out over a moonlit Welsh landscape, weighing it all up.

The seismic event in Shane's life, that schoolyard fight, had happened more than a year previously. Subsequent courses in anger-management must have been as baffling to a schoolboy as the phenomenon of the shine to the medical profession. Clifford had been unable to provide answers, but in the four months before Wales he and the boy had got on well. When he suggested the trip to Shane's Mom she agreed surprisingly easily. He had expected her to be reticent about letting her son scarper around Wales with a thirty-five year old man. When he mentioned that he often went there with Simon, his own eleven year old - whenever he could persuade Becky to let him go at half terms and other holidays - that seemed to clinch it. Shane's mother needed the break. A whole week without Shane was the best offer she'd had in twelve long months of heartache. He wanted a chance to test his theory.

Clifford had begun the search for chance patterns in the reports. According to the files, Boy 121's first outburst came after lessons in the specialist computer room at school. So had two of the next four school-based incidents. Hardly a convincing pattern. When Clifford read in a teacher's report that, on the morning of the third outburst, Shane had been working for half an hour on the PC in the corner of the classroom, he sat up so straight he strained his back. He slumped down when he realised there was no computer contact on the fourth day. That set him off on a hunting trip through aspects of Shane's life that seemed irrelevant. Background noise, for instance.

By now Mom was so frazzled she barely raised an eyebrow when he asked about the radio. On all the time, she said. What stations, what programmes, prior to and during the incidents? Half the times she could not remember. Clifford grilled her long enough to get a good idea of her radio habits. Checking programme listings he figured out what Shane was being bombarded with. He also got a fairly clear picture of TV exposure and noted how it, too, may have been responsible for flipping Shane into shine mode. Computers were more problematic. By jumpcutting into Shane's mood swings, Clifford became convinced they were also a stimulant.

The teenager on top of Snowdon had set Shane off again, not because his radio was too loud but because he had brought something back into Shane's brain that had not been there for most of a week. A faraway look came over Clifford's face as he recalled six idyllic days when Shane had regained his former self. The radio incident on Snowdon provided the final piece in the puzzle: sensory overload brought about by close proximity to the source. Maybe cellular phones could trigger it. Clifford thought of testing his mobile on Shane but thought better of it. Staring that long Welsh night at leaves rustling in moonlight, he concluded that Shane had a dangerous portal in his head. Something had seeped through, something fashioned of all the microwave radiation, net traffic, downloads, uploads, gygabytes, megabytes, analog and digital broadcasts, radio waves... It had sneaked through the portal. If it had seeped into Shane's head it could affect others, too.

He tried to explain this to Shane's Mom. She took it into her mind that Dr Clifford was blaming her for the boy's upbringing. She also jumped to the conclusion that he was mad. Worryingly, she felt he might persuade social services to take Shane from her. She broke off all contact and denied him access to her son.

Two weeks later Shane sat at the kitchen table, staring vacantly at the TV while the radio jabbered merrily in the background. He flung his plate at the wall. Mom turned around, startled. She saw the most vindictive shine ever. Pulsing with menace, the boy tried to scream. No sound came except a half-whimper to remind her of the puppies they used to keep but had to get rid of for their own protection. Shane jumped to his feet and kicked his chair back. He made as if to whip something off the table but Mom had learned to put away all the tablecloths months ago. Convulsing with rage, Shane lifted his end of the table and flipped it over. That brought the wettest, reddest, sweatiest shine his Mom had ever seen, a nova of rage and pain all over his face. Amid her pitiful screams he put his hands to his head as if to cover his ears. By the time she realised what was happening the brain aneurysm had him on the floor. He was stone cold dead.

Dr Matt Clifford was a man in a hurry. He swished past his secretary. "Sort out the files on my desk," he hissed, grabbing his coat. The elevator spilled him onto the ground floor. Before long he was on London streets, hailing a cab. The driver would need to put his foot on it to get him to Shane's service.

Clifford arrived with time to spare. The coffin was still open, leaving a chance for one last look at the child. The aneurysm had left no trace except the shine, diminished to pink, embellished by the whiteness of the shroud. With his golden hair still plastered to his forehead as much in death as in life, the pink shine lent a cherubic quality to Shane's face that was distinctly at odds with the mayhem, and ultimate death, it brought to his brain.

The undertakers caught Mom's eye. They screwed on the lid and wheeled the coffin outdoors into the hearse. The cemetery was just around the corner.

Matt Clifford remained a discreet distance from the graveside. He stood among a small knot of adults that included the headmaster and a group of teachers from Shane's school. There were no children. He sighed and looked skyward. Perhaps the school governors were right to keep nine year olds away from their classmate's funeral. Maybe they were wrong. No right or wrong exists in such circumstances, only sadness and loss.

Swaying autumnal trees shed gold and red offerings in the gusting wind. Clifford shuddered at how he would cope if his own son were to die so tragically. That brought a swelling to his throat and a need to rub his eyes. Falling leaves reminded him of that night in Wales, of that week when Shane found contentment. Perhaps the boy had been a surrogate for Simon. He thought again of their last night in Bala, of Welsh oaks silhouetted in moonlight, of piecing it all together.

There was no proof. Clifford had been hoping that the autopsy might reveal something. A quick call to the coroner's office confirmed that nothing unusual had shown up except a shadow on the brain. Some earlier scans had thrown up shadows, too. There was nothing definitive about this final one. Chemical imbalances caused shadows. What caused the chemical disturbances was the key to the mystery. If dissection of Shane's brain proved fruitless how could he prove anything?

A strong gust whipped leaf-devils across an open grave. The diggers lowered him now, easing ropes into the ground. More leaves came, small ones from nearby bushes, converging on the grave as if raining petals. They wanted to fall in, to spiral down and sleep with Shane, to be buried on him and with him, to comfort him and lend him fragrance and keep him company in the dark eternal night.

Two days later Clifford sat on a bench in Regent's Park. It was Saturday morning. Becky was due to let go of Simon for the weekend. Reluctantly, of course. She was late as usual.

A glass-shattering scream pierced Clifford like a dagger. He glanced behind to see a curly-haired girl of four or five shrieking and stomping the ground. At her foot an ice-cream cone bled streaky white lumps onto green grass. A young lady, possibly the girl's nanny, tried to reason with her but the child was having none of it. People were staring and smiling those special smiles they have for cute-but-misbehaving little children. Flustered, the nanny pulled her charge along the path carefully dodging furious ankle-kicks from the red-faced girl.

Nanny and child were soon out of sight behind trees. Clifford still heard the screams. He hoped that the girl's face was shiny with rage only. Perhaps he ought to have got up off the bench to find out where she lived, to follow-up on her in case the tantrum had been caused by something else. But Becky and Simon were on the path and at his side almost before he knew it.

"Sunday at six," she said, turning. She was on her way then. Not even the civility of a common greeting. Typical.

"Hi, Dad."

"Hello, Si." Clifford looked his son in the face a tad more intensely than usual.

Lost Notes

Aengus's eyes momentarily widened with alarm. Too wrapped up in childish things to notice that I had steered off the road merely to park, his gaze returned to normal as the wheels of the jeep settled into the soft roadside.

Anyone watching would have thought we were to spend the afternoon in pursuit of fish. Rods in the air, tackle bags on our shoulders, we left the jeep and walked past uniform lines of fertilizer bags puffing out their chests with turf. To our left, a solitary snipe strained its neck and stared at us with beady eye and long straight bill. It knew we were not fishing for fish, but then snipes know everything. I broke eye-contact with the bird and walked on. The wind rose, so did the land. I looked up fearing showers, but the western sky was clear. The hill was steep - steeper for smaller feet.

"How much further?" asked Aengus.

"Not far."

I took his hand as we jumped over a turf-walled trench deep as a grave. Not easy for him, not easy for his father either, plodding over sods that concealed ankle-twisting holes. Bog-cotton waves prettily, beneath it the detritus of ten thousand years opens up. Not easy, rods in hand, bags around neck - balance comes hard, breath comes hard. A stream gurgled to our right. It should not have been to our right. I hoped it was not that stream, the one we should be keeping to our left. Crest of hill confirmed that it was.

A blue-brown lake slid into view as if some unknown god had pushed out a massive, panoramic drawer from the wedge of hill beneath our feet. The drawer contained a mirror sparkling between mountainy folds of heather. My eyes soaked it up. I knew that more than nature was at work here. Magic permeated the air - not the cheap, illusory tricks of gameshow conjurors, but magick. I breathed in great lungfuls of it. It seeped, percolated, inebriated - in, through, up, down - filling my senses until I looked at the lake and knew for certain that down in its dark underbelly, something waited.

Loch Natragh, *Loch na Traigh,* Lake of Beaches. Two of them, small and white-sanded, lay at the eastern end. Separated by the merest spit of bogland, they may as well have been miles away. Correct stream, wrong side. To our right an impenetrable gorge; rhododendroned, steep-sided, not for adults much less children.

Below us a marshy bank. Heads bowed predaceously, we slinked to within casting distance. A trout rose invitingly. I ignored the fish and cast out quickly. My red rose sunk and snagged. I stood up straight and pulled it free. It snagged again - too many rushes spoiled the retrieve. Eventually I reeled in my ragged flower and glared at the rushes. Then I looked at Aengus. He was waiting to be rigged up. I glanced at the rushes once more. "Let's go," I nodded to the western end. "Looks clearer down there."

He shrugged and sighed a little.

"Best find a good spot before settling down," I added con-solingly.

Ours was a circuitous route because we had to climb anoth-er hill, a reed-infested quagmire down by the shore saw to that. Footholds were difficult, solidity a rare commodity in these parts. I heard Aengus's ragged breath behind me. It matched his jerky steps. When I heard him struggle no more I looked and saw it was because he could not keep up. I waited for him. He soldiered on gamely, once or twice catching me with that famil-iar look which asks why I have to do this, or more to the point, why he has to do it. I had no answer to that, so I turned around and marched on.

Ten paces later we reached the top of the hill. With no warn-ing the ground jumped up a metre. Luckily, only one of my legs dive-bombed into the bog-hole, otherwise who knows what depth I may have plumbed. I pulled my sore, sodden leg out of the morass and smiled ruefully at Aengus. I checked for damage to the rod and reel that fell with me, and looked down at the lake. "Damn," I muttered, cursing my eyesight - rushes were abundant here as well. I should have seen them sooner. Now we faced a hard slog around the far side. "There," I used my welling-ton as a pointer while I emptied it of water, "about halfway along, there's a place we can cast from."

My steps were prudent now, not just so Aengus could keep up. The terrain was firmer on this side. Huge folds of peat cor-rugated the land, making walking difficult. Stiffness slithered up my legs. Aengus's breath was still jerky, not entirely from exer-tion. "Nearly there now," I told him, knowing that his irritability was justified. I promised him milk and chocolate, and told him joyously that the water was free of reeds. Soon we reached the chosen spot. I checked my watch. Forty-five minutes since we stepped from the jeep.

I gave him sustenance, cast my line, and rigged him up. By the time he had made his cast I looked for my bubble float. It was not there. Hope fluttered briefly, then sank. The wind had merely blown the float back to the shoreline.

We cast our bubbles with roses attached - he with three, I with two. When he had finished his refreshments I broke the dreaded news. "It's no use, Aengus, the elements are against us here. Our flowers keep floating back in. Down on those beaches, we'd have no problem. The wind would carry our bait out far." With trepidation I mentioned this for I was fearful that all our setbacks might turn my son against that which I must teach him to do. But the sustenance strengthened him and he reeled in compliantly. Anyway he knew I would not rest until we were in the right place.

Ten more grudging minutes took us to where we should have been in the first place. Now we stood on a little white beach, wind at our backs. I rigged us both up, carnations this time - we had learned that rose petals disintegrated too readily in these conditions. Aengus cast ten metres; I twice that. Length did not matter as the wind carried our flowers out.

We stood on the beach for an hour casting and waiting. Occasionally our bait grew soggy and slipped beneath the surface. Wet carnation, slowly sinking, sometimes works - but not here. We tried different colours: pinks, reds, whites. Nothing took but we were patient, knowing the object of our pursuit was wary, nervous, and utterly unpredictable.

Aengus no longer asked the time. He came under a spell and so did I - the beauty of our surroundings guaranteed it. No trace of man here; no roads, no fences. Only God's own mountain, lake and bog - and man and boy.

Time passed. The sky turned kinder. Clouds chased higher, whiter. No threat of rain now, the wind died as Lake of Beaches became Lake of Glass. Even birdsong ended. A stillness came. It took the wildness from the wilderness and replaced it with an anticipation not conducive to small-talk. The world was pregnant now, and the time was near.

I lay my rod upon the sand, forgetting about the beautiful invitation sinking beneath my float. Nature, magick, prayer invaded my spirit. I felt renewed, at one with the universe, at peace with the world. Invisible to Aengus, I shook off the shackles of the world the way a newly-hatched mayfly shakes the water from her wings.

Aengus noticed it first. "Father!" he shouted. "Look!"

Nothing raises the weary spirit, nothing lifts the sinking heart, like the sight and sound of a line going taut. It whipped across the surface like a waterboatman gone mad. It shot out into the middle of the lake, a tiny wake spreading behind it. The rod-tip strained before I could bend to reach. It jerked toward the water before my hand was on it. I grabbed the butt-end just in time, striking quickly. In my fingers that glorious feel, that momentary resistance which signifies but one thing. I reeled in furiously. It fought a little - a living force, an elemental weight - I could sense it thinking about diving back into the darkness. Then it surrendered.

My son stood to the wrong side, net in hand. He has a lot to learn. Wary of losing momentum, and my catch, I decided not to waste time asking him to move to the correct position. "I'm going to beach it," I yelled, knowing it was very close.

The lake exploded two metres out. Something golden broke the surface, then disappeared as I pulled hard on the rod and gave the reel one last, mad twirl.

It erupted onto the beach in a fiery cascade of water and sand. There it lay flat, gasping and helpless as a premature baby. Aengus dropped to his knees and huddled over it. Overwhelmed with curiosity, he scanned it up and down with great swoops of his eyes. Unable to take his gaze from it, he asked, "What is it?"

I plucked the carnation from its golden-brown head and watched its azure wings stir a little. I lifted and separated them, blowing lightly. Aengus looked at me this time. With a great gulp of breath he demanded to know.

"Listen," I whispered, and the wings began that frantic, flapping action of the newborn. "Just listen," I whispered again, and he did.

I gently lifted the golden creature from the sand. A tremor ran through it and through me. Aengus and I knelt on the shore, my arms offering a frail, nascent gift to the fading light of day. I stretched up my hands to the sky above, to the red orb of the sun, and to the stars beyond. I bent my head in worship. Aengus instinctively, respectfully, did the same. In the palm of my hand a tiny heart beat.

The weight lifted from my palms and soared into the sky. More than rhythm to its wings now, the creature sang as it flew. There was music. Sacred music. At once new, forever ancient, it filled the mountains with notes of serene beauty. It redefined the space between mountains. Its resonance plumbed the depth of the lake, rebounded below, and echoed back up with a cosmic sonar that broke the surface and made our hearts tremble. Its chords would have felled trees if there had been trees here. A song to die for, it made the setting sun go slowly supernova until its burgeoning orb reached out, finger-pointing us with bright, red rays. The ground trembled beneath us, the lake shimmered as if a giant plectrum had come from somewhere and played the landscape.

All too soon it was gone, free, released. The bearer of trebles to make us tremble, of base notes to touch the hiding places of our minds, had soared so high its notes were lost in cloud. The music faded, the chorus ended, and the sun's glorious rays diminished as the sun itself slipped behind the mountain.

"I know what it is!" Aengus got off his knees and jumped up and down, as if jumping might bring him nearer to the sky and he might hear the lost notes again. "It's a song!" he yelled. "We caught a song!"

Reluctantly from Lough Natragh we trudged. Mindful of bog-holes, mindful of music beyond compare, we made our way to the jeep without mishap. Aengus was full of mountains, lakes and exotic creatures that sing as they fly. In his eyes I saw a look which told me he would spend his life forever in search of that which we released today. For that I was glad, for someone will have to take over from me when I am gone. I knew then that Aengus would be that person, and that is as it should be for he is my son.

But we were back in the realm of humankind with all its frailties and distractions. We drove on tar steamrolled long ago, past electricity wires long since hung, down to a wider road. There we joined a stream of red tail-lights wandering aimlessly through a concrete environment. We came at last to a driveway. No lakes or mountains here, but at least our home is surrounded by a rampart of broadleafed trees.

Aengus ran to the figure in the doorway, the story gushing from him. "We caught a song!" he yelled. His mother smiled and patted his head. Then she took him into the kitchen, heated his supper, and listened patiently while I went over to the yard to put the rods away. By the time his story was over I was bolting the shed. Before I had time to turn I heard the discreet click of the backdoor latch. My wife stepped out. She checked that the latch was secure before walking across the yard. I knew from her look that she had news. I do not know how she knows these things, she always does and is never wrong.

"There was a suicide off the bridge," she whispered. "A young girl."

"When?" I asked, knowing her answer.

"Before sunset." She put her hand on my shoulder and lifted her head. Together we looked up. Clouds had gone and there were stars.

I like to think a new star shone that night, the light of a soul released. But there were too many lights to count. I like to think that the music Aengus and I heard out at the lake was played by

Gabriel on his horn, or by the angels on their harps, and that the vocals were the joyous notes of a soul singing in celebration. I silently thanked the stars for giving me the key to unlock these tortured souls, and I put my arm around my wife. We stood there stargazing, secure in the knowledge of our destiny and our task, and secure in the knowledge that there was someone to follow us. Enough for us now to hear him sweetly singing in the kitchen, and enough for him, at his tender age, to think we are merely the fishers of songs.

SWANSONG

Out of the sun they came, awesome, a military formation at five o'clock. Barrett envied their fixed-wing certainty, their steadfast undercarriage. "They always use the same flight path," he said as he watched them adjust the angle of their feet for landing.

"Until they build the motorway," said Mbabi.

Barrett took in both sides of the estuary with a sweep of his eyes. To the south, a huge claw had gouged the countryside wide open. Here and there in the deep brown wound, yellow husks of diggers and other bits of machinery stood silent and passive in Sunday afternoon stillness. To the north, flyover pilings already in place, the first predatory concrete jutted like a jaw over the swan's flight path.

The birds glided to a halt, bow waves rippling the reeds. "Let me show you one of their nests." He took Mbabi by the hand. "The male gathers the material but it's the female who builds it."

"The way it should be," Mbabi grinned. "Men for strength, women for brains."

Barrett let that pass. Together they tiptoed as close as they dared. When they reached that demarcation line known only to swans, where the cob started to hiss, they backed off.

Over a meal in a roadside pub an hour later, Mbabi said, "Why didn't you bring your cameras?"

"Too much like work. I've taken hundreds of swan shots, way too many."

"I still cannot believe the size of that nest, so large. It was so out in the open, so..." Seeking the right word, her brow furrowed with lines perpendicular to the strips of russet dye that streaked her short curly hair from back to front.

"Arrogant?" Barrett shook his head. "Swans are not like that. Regal maybe, not arrogant. That's the thing about birds. Their sense of purpose is one-dimensional. They're like little engines driven by instinct. Take the swans. It's their nature to be regal. They have to be. That's the difference between birds and domestic animals. Pets in houses have their own agendas. Cats use you and dogs depend on you, but birds live for the moment. They're like little bundles of energy wild and free - totally upfront, nothing undercover."

The red-black plumage of Mbabi's hair, her delicate eyes and vividly lined smile put a spell on Barrett. She was as rare as a golden oriole in the city, but more precious.

"We'd better hurry." She checked her watch. "I'm on duty at seven. I'll be hung out to dry if I'm late."

"Babby, your English is so good you're using idioms to beat the band."

"Pardon?"

Barrett smiled at her nervous, agitated look. The look that came whenever something perplexed her.

*   *   *

Barrett stopped his car on the brow of the hill by the hospital entrance. A jeep drove past, the fifth army vehicle he had seen since morning. They were on the streets like buses these days - you never saw one without another. A second jeep careened around the corner.

Mbabi broke his thoughts. "I'm not the only one who's late," she nodded in the wake of the army vehicles, promising to text him when her shift was over. She got out of the car, flitting away on the breeze, leaving Barrett with a half empty, half full feeling.

He drove home, parked, and stood in his hallway scratching his chin. A shave could wait till morning. He walked past the swan photo on his living room wall trying not to let it catch his eye. He did not want to be drawn into it, not when he wanted to dwell on how much Mbabi meant to him. He *should* have explained his gift that afternoon, or alluded to it in some way. The swans in the estuary were a tailor-made excuse for saying something but he was afraid she might think him mad and he might lose her. He sighed. Despite himself, he stood with his back against the living room wall, staring across the room. He let the swan picture work its magic. In its mysterious way it pulled him in, drawing his eyes from the main image of two white swans on black water to that V-shaped flight of geese in the top left-hand corner. As ever, they flew into the middle of the picture.

He was away, an only child lying on his bed gazing wide-eyed at his favourite picture in his favourite book. A motorboat called the *Suzy Q* cut a V-shaped wake in the middle of a bright blue sea surrounded by a four-funnelled liner, tugboats and fire-fighting ships. Fish jumped, the fire ships saluted the liner with huge fountains of salt-white spray. In that picture there had been a flock of birds flying in formation like the old-fashioned orna-mental geese on the chimneybreast of the council house where he lived. The chimneybreast was in the room downstairs, a room full of familiar shouting, the room where father slapped mother with the side of his hand again and again. Barrett stuffed his fingers into his seven-year old ears and tried with all his might to keep out the shouting, the screaming. He concentrated hard on the *Suzy Q*, longing to be in that picture. To a frightened lonely schoolboy it seemed the only method of escape. Someday soon, he hoped, its little engine would take him sailing far, far away...

Ever since those days Barrett had sought refuge in his own imagination. His upbringing bestowed on him the mischievous ability to dive into pictures. In later life, he succeeded in transferring this through the camera. His mind could jump through the diaphragm, past the lens, into whatever lay beyond. This led to a life-long fixation with photography. Right through teenage years into adulthood he demanded to be true to his art. He loved photographing birds more than anything else. Something about the gift of flight captivated him. This other gift, that of entering photographs and *changing* them, had developed only in adulthood. Nowadays the gift seemed to be taking on extra texture, extra depth, as if it was evolving, morphing into some new manifestation that thrilled and scared him at the same time. He had often thought that perhaps it had all started with that picture of the *Suzy Q* and the birds flying overhead.

The phone rang, jolting Barrett from a childhood that haunted him. It was Moroney from the office. "Get your camera out to the back road at Pollenstown Golf Club," he barked. "They're in a field behind the ninth green."

"What are?"

"Corpses. At least half a dozen of them."

Next morning Barrett stood in the editor's office demanding to know why the paper was not publishing his photo of the victims.

"It's too graphic," said Moroney.

"I've heard it all now. This is supposed to be a hard-hitting newspaper."

"It's not a tabloid."

"You think publishing a shot of eight bullet-sprayed, blood-drenched corpses is beneath us?"

Moroney sighed and looked sideways out the window, a hint of moustache beneath his hooked beak. "Your photo wasn't prioritised at the morning meeting."

"I don't believe that."

"No other paper is going with it. Check around if you like."

"That's because none of the others were let near the field. They were kept well away. I only got the shot 'cause I crept up through the golf course."

"You did what?" Moroney looked like Roadrunner scratching his head.

"My instinct told me not to approach directly. I played there a couple of times. I know my way to the ninth green in the dark."

"Amazing what golf leads to."

"Eight people are dead! Gunned down by the looks of it, their corpses guarded by soldiers while troops spilled out of APC's and kept the rest of the press out on the road. You think that doesn't merit the front page?"

"Like I said, we have other things to go with." Moroney sat on his perch behind his desk and picked up a sheaf of papers.

Barrett looked down at his boss. Rays of morning sun slanted through the window, lighting a glare on Moroney's bald head - an effect that would have been funny were it not for the sly career-climbing brain ticking away beneath it. "You've been nobbled, haven't you?" said Barrett. "Someone got to you last night."

The editor lifted his head and squared up to Barrett with the cold keen eyes of a bottom feeder. "Your contract is up in two months. If you're not careful, you might be taking your lenses elsewhere, and your awards. Pity last night's picture will be stale by then."

Barrett swooped out of the newspaper offices and walked the police-ridden streets all day. An albatross twisted and looped in his brain. It was not the swan picture that plagued him now. In the lens-eye of his mind he saw the corpses. He saw their blood. Zooming in, he saw their faces.

Twenty-four hours after being hissed from the swan's nest, Mbabi lay in Barrett's arms on the couch in his apartment. "Won't another paper publish it?" she asked.

"It's not that easy." Barrett caressed her hair. "There are so many controls now. Okay if it's some celebrity-based story but not if it's anything political. Besides, I'm contracted to one paper only."

"Would you quit your job over this?"

Barrett glanced at the award-winning photo on the wall, the shot of the swan. In all the nights Mbabi had stayed he hadn't mentioned once that the award won by that photo had been his passport into photojournalism. He had pointed out the award to every other girl he had invited over, but not her. It was as if he didn't need to impress her in that way. In the cool dark water beneath the swan he saw a wobbly reflection of himself taking school portraits and shots of houses for auctioneers. That was one future he did not want. He looked at the cob swan, its graceful neck and clear eye.

Mbabi followed his gaze. "It's a stunning picture. I noticed it the first night I was here and meant to ask about it."

Barrett made as if to tell her something but said, "Sorry I never texted you. I was fuming after that meeting with Moroney. I never checked for messages." He looked into her eyes, dark like deep pools on a hot day.

"What is it? What's bothering you?" she said.

Barrett knew he could trust her. Secretive as a water-rail darting from thicket to thicket, and as easily alarmed, Mbabi was nothing if not careful. Months on the run across two continents had made her like that. Sometimes recollections came back to haunt her - memories of hopes de-railed in dingy freight yards; razor wire cutting her off from her own country, her own people; shabby doss houses and shady deals; container ports and thirty-six hours in a sweat-metal coffin that stank of piss and shit. Sometimes the memories resurfaced in her face as brightly as if some policeman shone his torch at her, as many did in railway stations across North Africa and Europe.

Barrett saw all the secret policemen in all the world, some not so secret. They stood over her as she tried to sleep at night, shining slimy torches, illuminating the purple pigmentation of her face, lighting up the dreams and secrets in her head. Their vertical white beams like stalactites ready to fall and pierce her fragile skin. He pulled her close and whispered. "It's the photo. It was dark so I can't be sure... Two of the corpses were face down. As far as I can tell from the flesh tones of faces and hands, and I've studied the shot through all kinds of scans and filters, not one of the eight victims was white."

He felt her wince and pulled her closer. It was a lie, of course, about scans and filters. The camera in his mind had zeroed in through the darkness and showed him the colour of their faces. Still he could not reveal the secret of his gift to her, at least not yet.

For days Moroney's shifty presence hung over the office like a hawk in an updraft. The editor was getting on everybody's nerves, especially Barrett's. There were people in the newspaper he could talk to but no one he could confide in. He felt fear and paranoia incubate within him. How do you shaft a boss when everyone else is in cahoots with him? Barrett felt naked and helpless, his every move observed as if someone had construct-ed a hide outside his window. The barrels of unseen lenses warmed his neck every time he moved.

The streets towered over him as he walked home. Buildings that promised freedom, knowledge, enlightenment - libraries, galleries, museums - had for more than a year been changing their tones from light to dark. It was a subtle alteration, invisible to most. The pace of change had accelerated in recent months. People had not noticed, but Barrett knew that some morning they would wake up to find their office towers and apartment blocks leaning like neglected tombstones, blocking light and hope, ready to fall and bury them in darkness. Barrett could sense it everywhere: restriction and constriction closing in like the talons of a condor on a lamb.

That night he and Mbabi went to a club and drank too much. They hatched plans of migration to somewhere warm and welcoming. At 5am, as they nested in each other's arms in bed, the phone rang.

Moroney. Another assignment.

Clouds were cracked with sunlight to the east. A steady breeze cut from the same direction. The wind and morning smells of a moist field could not quell the stale tobacco rising from Barrett's jacket. It drifted into his nostrils like clandestine smoke, clinging to him the way dew clings to grass. The rigidity of the stalks through the thick soles of his shoes told him this was not grass but stubble of corn or wheat. Whatever they grew here was a mystery to him, a city boy.

He jumped at a flutter of wings in the trees to his left. A murder of crows took flight. Beyond the wheeling birds, the distant spires of town. Beneath them the club where he and Mbabi had spent too much of the previous night. The cameras around his neck weighed extra heavy. Breathing was hard as if testifying to his lack of fitness. It was not easy, watching the world through eyes hooded with drink from the night before. Low winter sun was no help especially when walking straight into it. He could still hear the cawing of the crows. A dog howled somewhere in middle distance, its plaintive cry lost in the squelch of mud around his feet. At least most of the mud lay behind him as the field began to rise.

He tried to walk between stalk stubbles. His consolations were that his hangover had often been worse, this was his first assignment in days, and he was almost at the crest of the field. He knew what he would find on the other side. Bodies, police. He hoped that by coming this long way round he might once again beat the other photographers to the best shot. Out of breath, with the sun making misery of his eyes, he stood on the brow of the field and looked down. His legs suddenly weighed a thousand tons. He was staring at the one thing he did not want to see.

The wrong uniforms.

Dozens of army men surrounded a large white crime lab tent. Barrett knew it was the scene of another execution. A mass execution if the size of the tent was a guide. His eyes blinked at one-thousandth of a second. In a flash he saw what lay inside the tent. The vision rooted him to the spot like a zombie caught in headlights. This was a new and unexpected aspect of his gift. Not only could he see strange things in photos, he could see through physical barriers. Stunned as he was, the pro in him took over. He just had to get the picture. Like a true photographer facing a charging elephant, he instinctively lifted his camera and focused. With all the f-stops his camera - or his mind, he wasn't sure which - could muster he reeled off four shots.

He heard the soldiers shouting at him from their half-track as they made their way uphill. They cured his astonishment at what he had seen with the threat of guns. They bundled him aboard the half-track and sped off to the roadside where a jumped-up sergeant manhandled Barrett down onto the road and pointed him in the general direction of the city. "Fuck off back to the rest of the snoops, you stupid hack," snapped the sergeant, who neglected to smash Barrett's cameras because, for all he knew, Barrett's only crime was to photograph the side of a large white tent.

"How on Earth did you get this?" Moroney glared at the image.

He seemed even more fidgety than usual, reminding Barrett of a house martin whose chicks have gone missing from the nest.

"Never mind how. I got it. That's all that matters. All the other papers will only have a big white tent. Are we going to print it?"

Moroney rubbed hard on the nape of his neck. Barrett could see that his editor's tail would have been wagging conspicuously, had he had a tail.

"No," chirped Moroney. "Definitely not. There's been a directive."

Mbabi regarded her boyfriend with that elusive, nocturnal look he found so attractive.

"It's true, Babby. I see things in cameras and photos. I can change them, take them, even see through them with my mind's eye."

She arched slowly back from his embrace.

"I'm telling the truth. You're in danger. We're all in danger. People are being murdered wholesale. Especially foreigners."

He wanted to explain it properly. How the gift seeped into his sleep, ate into his dreams. The way it had started and what it had led to. How it was progressive, mutant, evolving into visions that were dangerous, threatening to tear him apart. The chronology in cold, got-to-be-believed matter-of-factness. He had rehearsed it. How it was no longer a gift, more of an affliction. The words had either deserted him or else they sounded stupid. Stupid beyond belief. In Mbabi's eyes he saw the tops of tears. He also saw that familiar perplexed look that made his heart jump with fear that she might slip away. With every millimetre that she backed off he saw only too clearly that all the hope and love she had invested in him was ebbing like a spring tide. There was nothing he could do.

She stood rock still, imperious as a heron.

In a glimpse Barrett re-lived the day he first met her. She

stood among the rocks gathering periwinkles to sell to a local restaurant. He was walking along the beach, snapping waders. Their eyes met and nothing was ever the same. He became her one bright light in an alien landscape. Not any more. "Won't you even let me hold you?" he pleaded, standing very steady as if sudden movement might frighten her. Neither moved for one long moment. She answered his question by backing further away until she was out of arm's reach. He could see then the whole of her tears as away she flew, out through the apartment door, lost to the skies forever.

In the dismal days that followed, Barrett knew that if Mbabi didn't believe him nobody would. If she thought he was insane so would everyone. How could he talk to his colleagues about his crazy gift? It was a no win scenario. If he failed to provide photographic evidence no one would believe him. If he did provide it, they would put it down to camera-trickery or digital manipulation. He thought long and hard, then turned up for work and surprised Moroney by requesting a routine assignment to take standard shots at the annual passing-out parade at Central Barracks. "Yes, yes," warbled Moroney, restless as ever.

Barrett flashed his pass at the perimeter gates and walked in. His heart thumped like a hummingbird's in a net. Within the barrack walls he felt scared and threatened like a nestling wandering about a valley beneath the hungry gaze of eagles. Somehow he held his camera steady in palms shiny from sweat and reeled off the required shots. He could not get out quickly enough. Never was any man so glad to escape the clutches of an army now so all-pervasive that almost all aspects of life were under military control, including newspapers. It had all happened so quickly. The journey from democracy to military control had taken less than a week.

Moroney, delighted by Barrett's enthusiastic request to cover the passing-out parade, though suspicious of his photographer's motives, approved a wide-angled shot for the front page.

Early next morning, in newsagents everywhere, shop assistants were puzzled to see a small amount of red ink seeping from bundles of one particular broadsheet. Snipping open the morning delivery, they realised to their horror that the liquid oozing from the papers was blood, the same sad helpless blood that had gushed from the thirty massacred corpses hidden from view behind that white crime lab tent. Now the victims lay in open view, three lines of ten, flat on the parade ground. Just a thimble of their blood dripping from each photo where they lay in front of proud new soldiers.

Every hard copy of the newspaper was similarly affected. Even the online edition did not escape. Loggers-on contacted their PC hotlines complaining of a mysterious red toner-like substance that smeared their fingers if they touched the onscreen photo.

Within half an hour the snatch squad came for Barrett. They battered his door down, barged through his hallway into his living room, knocking his award-winning swan photo off the wall. Its glass frame smashed into pieces as it hit the floor, a flight of birds with broken wings. They ransacked his apartment as if he also had the ability to miniaturize himself but they did not find him there. He was loose in the city, running for his life.

Whatever self-preservational instincts worked in Barrett's head, they deserted him in his final hours of freedom. He had no place to lay low. His mind whirled with the craziness of it all. A once benign gift had progressed so much he could take photos through barriers - but what, he thought, if the image of the corpses behind the tent was not genuine? What if the corpses were not real? His mind zoomed in and showed him for the first time the faces of the victims in their three sad rows of ten. They were real enough. Some he recognised as well-known politicians and public figures. Others, he guessed, were faces of the homeless, the foreign, the disappeared. One face he knew too well. It was the last face to come clearly into focus. It was himself. Barrett clenched his fists so tight his fingernails dug into his own skin. He felt scared. He felt he was going mad. He felt tightness in his ribcage, dryness in his throat, his heart was beating a million to one.

He tried to steady his thoughts, to banish madness from his mind. He told himself he at least had a plan he had been wise enough to implement before this present lunacy threatened to take over his mind. Right now he felt as if his head was going to explode. He had enough sense to remember his scheme to get out, to get as far away as possible.

For some reason the prospect of flight had lured him irresistibly. He tried to look normal as he entered the airport terminal. He had booked a flight, under a false name, the morning of the passing-out parade. For an aeon-long instant the check-in clerk examined his papers before waving him through. Turning from the desk, Barrett thought he had made it. He could feel the wings unfurling on his back. When he saw the soldiers at the boarding gate he knew his luck would not hold.

With gaunt face and skewered heart he flashed his boarding card almost nonchalantly. The corporal pointed his gun and asked him to come for questioning. Barrett knew the game was up. The diaphragm in his mind opened to show him one last picture, a snapshot of what the troops would do. The final evolution of his bizarre gift showed him his own death. His heart dropped like a game-bird blasted full of lead.

With not a trace of irony in their faces they took him to the estuary where that concrete motorway jutted out over the swan's flight path like a jaw. Laughing, they frogmarched Barrett to a ledge. Looking down he could see a cavity soon to be filled by a bulk cement carrier. He could hear its engine idling, the driver grinning from his cab as he waited to dump his load on him. The troops stopped laughing as three soldiers stepped forward, nudging him with their guns.

A lot of thoughts converged in Barret's head. Moroney hovered somewhere nearby, he knew. He felt the ghosts of mother and father, still bickering after all these years. All his best photos flipped through his head. His last cogent thought was of Mbabi. He hoped she might escape. He prayed she would. He prayed for himself.

As the cavity floor rushed up to greet him, he saw with the gift of zoom vision, and heard with a strange new gift of dynamic hearing, his own swansong rise above everything. Swooping down, his spirit soared. In that moment he glimpsed a small motorboat in estuarine water, its engine spluttering in readiness to transport him to wherever boats like the *Suzy Q* might go. Overhead, a flight of something white flew in V-shaped formation, like a fly-past on some auspicious occasion. As darkness embraced him, he saw all his photos, every last one, and all the photos ever taken in the history of the whole world, every last one dripping with blood and smelling of sweat and fear, all framed with gun barrels that reeked of smoke and oil, and he hoped it might not come true.